MW00986586

Praise for
The Night Library of Sternendach

"Revel in every turn of phrase in this lyrical, classical romance of Kunigunde Heller, trapped between her family and tradition, and her own desires kindled under the starry sky in *The Night Library of Sternendach*."

—Margaret S. McGraw, co-editor of *Lawless Lands* and *Predators in Petticoats*

"Lévai debuts with a lush, modern take on the trope of supernaturally star-crossed lovers...This operatic love story caters to many beloved tropes while providing a fresh perspective and building toward an unusual, bittersweet ending that explores 'how love costs more than it seems.'"

—*Publishers Weekly*

"A stunning achievement in storytelling and the poetic form....I can't wait to read more."

—Emily Leverett, co-editor of *Predators in Petticoats*

"Gorgeously romantic in both style and story. Lévai's timeless tale will sweep you off your feet with immortal dealings and human emotion."

—Matthew Vesely, author of *Elegy for the Undead*

The Night Library of Sternendach

A Vampire Opera in Verse

by Jessica Lévai

LANTERNFISH PRESS

PHILADELPHIA

Lanternfish Press
399 Market Street #360
 Philadelphia, PA 19106

lanternfishpress.com

Cover Design: Kimberly Glyder

Printed in the United States of America.
Library of Congress Control Number: 2020941235
Print ISBN: 978-1-941360-51-4
Digital ISBN: 978-1-941360-52-1

Contents

1955

Prologue

1967

Act I: Idyll
Act II: Complications
Act III: Revelations
Act IV: Betrayals
Act V: Choices

Dramatis Personae

The vampires:

THE GRAF OF STERNENDACH, *baritone*

AMATA, his Gräfin, *soprano*

TIMOCH, his retainer and bodyguard, *bass*

The humans:

LUZIA HELLER, current leader of the Heller family of vampire hunters, also called "Oma", *mezzo-soprano*

EVA, her daughter-in-law, *contralto*

KUNIGUNDE, Eva's daughter, Luzia's granddaughter, also called "Kinge", *mezzo-soprano*

GALEN, The Graf's familiar and the Gräfin's lover, *tenor*

MARIA and **ATHANASIUS HELLER**, Luzia's mother and grandfather, are gone by the time of this story, but their memories linger in the hearts of those who knew them.

The Night Library
of Sternendach

A Vampire Opera in Verse

Prologue

1. By seven, Kunigund' saw plainly
    The burdens she would grow up with:
    Her name (romantic, if ungainly)
    And knowledge vampires weren't a myth.
    The Heller clan, for generations
    Had hunted such abominations.
    A very few were left alive
    That summer night in fifty-five
    When, at her grandmother's insistence,
    Her mother stuffed her in a new
    Pink dress, and Oma drove them to
    The castle looming in the distance.
    There she would meet, at eight o'clock,
    The vampire Graf of Sternendach.

2. Such visits are about tradition
    And not a pleasant social act.
    They satisfy but one condition
    Of many in a solemn pact.
    In eighteen ninety-seven, Hellers
    Slew Graf and Gräfin in their cellars.
    The new Graf, ruling in their stead,
    And wishing no more people dead,
    Proposed a compromise that stated
    No vampire might, to sate his needs,
    Cause death for those on whom he feeds.
    The Hellers, too, cooperated
    And as consideration, swore
    They'd not slay vampires any more.

3. The two sides signed a treaty, saying
    That anyone who breaks this peace
    Will find himself (or herself) paying
    A fatal price for that caprice.
    To keep this grim arrangement going,
    One extra thing is needed. Knowing
    The Hellers are but mortal, one—
    A woman—serves as liaison,
    Succeeded later by her daughter.
    The one who rules the fam'ly now
    Is eldest of this party: Frau
    Luzia Heller. She has brought her
    One grandchild up to be prepared
    To take a role she can't be spared.

4.   Luzia's mother, called Maria,
     First set these women on this path,
     Conceding to the Graf's idea
     To save her people from his wrath.
     This took no small amount of will: her
     Own father was the old Graf's killer.
     Luzia has her mother's hair;
     In all else, she's her grandsire's heir.
     More patient, though. More calculating.
     She knows her enemies by heart,
     Has mastered many weapons' art,
     And seldom smiles. Participating
     Despite her hatred seems a way
     Of keeping other pain at bay.

5.   Now, Eva, Kunigunde's mother,
     Her husband was Luzia's son.
     They loved their child and one another,
     But Eva's dreams were come undone
     The night he took his father driving
     And crashed, with neither one surviving.
     For Kunigunde, Eva stayed
     And tried to learn the fam'ly trade.
     Alas, she has no stomach for it.
     She firmly grips her daughter's hand
     And gives in to the Graf's demand
     To meet. She knows she can't ignore it,
     And wishes she had strength to fight.
     Someday she may, but not tonight.

6.   Amid this roiling fam'ly drama,
    Young Kunigunde chatters. "Does
    The castle have a princess, Mama?"
    She wants to know. What interest is
    Her Oma's spite, her mother's worry?
    The castle beckons—Hurry! Hurry!
    The last of sunset's golden glow
    Receding from the town below
    Is gone, but gets a grand revival
    As towers loom and turrets rise
    Against the star-strewn velvet skies.
    It dazzles her at their arrival.
    She gets one final look before
    They sweep her through the castle's door.

7.   They're not in yet. The room before them
    Is simple, well-secured, and small.
    An iron safe is waiting for them
    Behind a panel in the wall.
    The women, as is necessary,
    Remove the weapons which they carry
    As heirlooms and as points of pride
    And place the pistols safe inside.
    They do not carry stakes. Though charming,
    Their rustic, rough-hewn quality
    Ill suits the present century.
    Most hunters nowadays are arming
    Themselves with guns which, like as not,
    They load with custom wooden shot.

8.   These precious guns now locked securely
      Away, Luzia takes the key.
      "Good ev'ning, Timoch," she says. "Surely
      You'll come out now where we can see."
      He steps from out the shadow lightly.
      He greets Luzia, nods politely,
      Then shows the way with outstretched hand.
      The child knows Timoch is no man.
      A vampire, and the Graf's retainer,
      He's seen three hundred winters pass.
      And there's no fighter in his class,
      Her Oma says, though he looks plainer
      Than she'd have thought. A poor surprise,
      This vampire first to meet her eyes.

9.   Their footfalls echo in the quiet
      Of hallways lined with tapestries.
      A candle winks as they walk by. It
      Sends shadows dancing, and she sees
      The figures as alive. The glinting
      Of golden thread, its richness hinting
      At fairy-story opulence,
      Appeals to seven-year-old sense.
      When Timoch stands aside, revealing
      His Excellency's private suite,
      She almost cannot keep her feet.
      And yet it's not the painted ceiling,
      The draperies, or cornices
      That draw her gasp—for there he is.

10. If Timoch's only ordinary,
     His lord looks every inch the part
     Of vampire prince. His height, his very
     Demeanor serve to touch her heart
     With frost. He leans against a table,
     In formal suit of grey and sable
     With only one chromatic note:
     The red silk knotted at his throat.
     He turns toward them. Is she staring?
     Does she sense something just beneath
     His smile, which does not hide his teeth?
     He has a graceful, noble bearing,
     But Oma gave her this advice:
     There's none alive who's crossed him twice.

11. "Good ev'ning, ladies." (And his voice is
     As smooth as glass and just as fine.)
     "What can I offer you? Your choice is
     Some coffee, or perhaps some wine."
     Luzia is the first to answer:
     "I beg you, spare this courtly dance, sir.
     We understand why we are here,
     Since you required we appear."
     With narrowed eyes and sour expression,
     He says, "It is a true delight
     To have you in my home tonight."
     He softens. "Eva, you're a vision.
     How kind of you to come." But she
     Looks wistful at his courtesy.

12. "So this, at last, is Kunigunde,"
    The Graf says, in his silken tone.
    "Just seven years? It is a wonder
    How in such time the child has grown."
    Although his presence may have jarred her
    He kneels now, better to regard her,
    And asks for only her to hear,
    "How do you like my castle, dear?"
    It makes her feel a little braver,
    The gentle way he asks, and soon
    She sheds her diffident cocoon.
    His eyes upon her never waver.
    He listens to his youthful guest
    Describe the parts she likes the best.

13. "What's *that*?" she asks. The vampire rises
    And turns to look, then gives a laugh
    As he sees what so tantalizes
    The child: a volume bound in calf
    And tooled with gold. He reads the title,
    "*The Stars of Sternendac*h. A vital
    Retelling of our country's lore.
    Perhaps you've seen its like before?"
    He opens to an illustration
    Of knights and princesses below
    An astral vault, and bends to show
    It her. She nods appreciation
    But says to him, "And now I need
    To hold the book so I can read."

14. He hesitates, but she's insistent.
    He says, "Then take it for your own."
    Luzia's face shows she's resistant
    To this largesse their host has shown.
    She says, "If this concludes our meeting,
    You must excuse us. We'll be needing
    To take our Kinge home. It's late.
    Might Timoch lead us to the gate?"
    The Graf, ignoring her, releases
    The book to Kinge's eager hand
    And says to her, "Now, understand
    This work contains some favorite pieces
    Of mine. Enjoy them, little one.
    I'd like your thoughts when you are done.

15. "For now, good night and pleasant dreaming."
    And so her heart completes its thaw.
    She clasps her lovely present, beaming,
    Her fear of him transformed to awe.
    She curtseys, like her mother told her,
    And only once looks ov'r her shoulder
    To watch the Graf recede from view.
    Once Timoch leads her fam'ly through
    The halls, Luzia stops to gather
    Their weapons and, like that, it's done.
    The ride home is a silent one.
    A tired Kunigund' would rather
    Stay up to read, but in the car's
    Back seat she sleeps, and dreams of stars.

Idyll

1. It's Friday, and the day is dying
   (The summer, too, though not quite yet),
   The city's lamps and headlights vying
   To light the way once sun has set.
   Downtown the city stirs, awaking
   To second life, the people taking
   In food and friends in small cafés,
   Then off to shopping, concerts, plays.
   Through all this Kunigunde wanders.
   She soon starts university,
   But for a span of time, she's free
   To take the air. At times she ponders
   The castle perched above the sprawl
   That casts its shadow over all.

2.   Tonight, the castle and its master
      Should not be further from her mind.
      With Oma out of town, at last, her
      Unending lessons are consigned
      To later thought. She has collected
      Her auburn hair in unaffected
      And charming plaits. To match their sheen,
      A knee-length dress in em'rald green.
      She seeks a bistro's outdoor table,
      Where she can watch the crowds go by
      And, while she's at it, maybe try
      A sample of the local label.
      Once served, she to her seat adjourns
      And smiles at boys whose heads she turns.

3.   The Riesling and the boys' admiring
      Are satisfying. Passably.
      She'd hoped for something more inspiring,
      If not quite sure what that might be
      When setting out on this excursion.
      She itches for a new diversion.
      There is, if she remembers right,
      An opera being sung tonight.
      And opera houses, she is certain,
      Attract more worldly clientele,
      Well-dressed and more grown-up as well.
      She must arrive before the curtain!
      Abandoning her glass and chair,
      She hurries to the central square.

4. And as her footsteps bring her near, and
   Electric lights give way to gas,
   From concrete, cobblestones appear, and
   A fountain bubbles. Here they pass:
   The tourists and the opera's patrons
   (Substantial men and wealthy matrons).
   Their flashy clothes and jewelry seem
   Contrary to the antique gleam
   Of gaslight. Rising up behind them,
   The Opera, with its open doors,
   Admits the crowd, and in it pours.
   So elegant does Kinge find them,
   She stares a bit more than she ought,
   But doubts that this is what she sought.

5. At least the house itself impresses.
   Stone angels, gods, and horses fly,
   While grotesques haunt its arched recesses.
   The last of sunlight leaves the sky;
   The final opera-goers hasten
   Within the theater. From her place in
   The square she sees the lobby's light
   Before the doors are shut up tight.
   Then all is still. In what direction
   Should Kunigunde this time head?
   It's really much too soon for bed.
   She stands some minutes in reflection,
   Distracted then by something new:
   A black car purring into view.

6.   She knows this car. And all unbidden
     Her Oma's voice sounds in her ear,
     "You're out alone. Now get you hidden
     Before those creatures find you here."
     She doesn't move. Why ever would she?
     Twelve years it's been. The likelihood she
     Might chance upon them, here, tonight,
     Is far too small. She'll stay, all right.
     First out is Timoch, who emerges
     As plain of face as she recalls
     From meeting in the castle's halls.
     Next, Timoch from the back seat urges
     A stately vampire lady, gowned
     In amber silk, her blond hair wound

7.   About her head. This is Amata,
     Whom Kunigund' has never met.
     Nor 'til this moment had she got a
     Good look at her in person. Yet
     She'd recognize her from descriptions
     In Oma's records. Such inscriptions
     Tell little of her private life;
     In public, she's the Lord Graf's wife.
     Most any human she'd enamor,
     This lovely figure, draped in gold.
     To Kunigunde, it's a cold,
     Unearthly thing, this vampire glamour.
     Her training has made her immune,
     She thinks, of course, a bit too soon.

8. For when the Graf appears, it shakes her.
   If childishly her heart had warmed
   To him an age ago, it makes her
   Blush hot, to find her grown self charmed.
   As he glides t'ward his destination
   She watches, rapt in fascination
   And lets escape a tiny sigh.
   He stops, and turns, and meets her eye.
   No sound, no movement but the beating
   Within her breast between them now.
   He offers her a graceful bow.
   She awkwardly returns his greeting,
   Which draws from him a kindly smile.
   They watch each other for a while.

9. But then, they hear the opera starting.
   Faint music through the entry swells.
   The Graf smiles once again in parting
   And nods to Kunigund': Farewell.
   His Gräfin's pleasure now attending,
   He takes her arm in his. Ascending
   The Opera's stairs, they open wide
   A door and disappear inside.
   No moon tonight. The stars come slowly
   To dot the sky. Their panoply
   Stirs echoes in her memory,
   The images of something wholly
   Important she forgot, somehow.
   She must go home and find it. Now.

10. At first, when she was only seven,
     She always kept his gift nearby.
     But by the time she turned eleven,
     She had to read it on the sly
     Because Luzia confiscated
     The book and it was relegated
     To Oma's office down the hall.
     The iron safe within the wall
     Contains it still. Luzia gave her
     Permission to go in, if need
     Arose while she was gone. And she'd
     Be gone for weeks, with fortune's favor.
     She probably would never know.
     The hallway lights should stay off, though.

11. The swords on hangers seem to warn her;
     The clock ticks disapprovingly.
     The safe itself waits in the corner,
     Between displays of weaponry.
     But none of this sways her decision.
     She spins the dial with calm precision:
     Turn left, then right, then left again.
     (She's known the code since she was ten.)
     First, documents, as she expected.
     The Hellers' written history,
     All sorted chronologically
     And into sturdy files collected.
     She slides them carefully aside
     And reaches past them, deep inside.

12. She finds a case of lacquered metal.
     It's full of boxes, which contain:
     A handsome watch, a soldier's medal,
     A tiny cross upon a chain.
     Past all of these her fingers, shaking,
     Brush soft, familiar leather, taking
     Her volume out. The cover gleams
     Like stars in her forgotten dreams.
     And Kinge happily immerses
     Herself again in stories told
     Of princes who could weep pure gold
     And maidens fighting wicked curses,
     Exciting as they were before.
     But now, years later, she wants more.

13. She skims her Oma's compilation
     Of all they know about the Graf.
     It has but little illustration,
     And not a single photograph.
     The next file in the safe comprises
     A ream of notes she recognizes
     As from the Graf himself. His hand
     Is elegant, precise and grand.
     These letters document occasions
     Like when new vampires joined his ranks,
     Or transfers from his many banks
     To Heller coffers. Celebrations
     Are noted, too. He sent his best
     For weddings, and new babies blessed.

14. Long over all these notes she lingers,
     Retracing every line and stroke
     His pen had made, as if her fingers
     Could with their own his touch invoke.
     The mem'ry of their meetings haunts her,
     And obstacles between them daunt her,
     But soon a plan begins to brew.
     She takes the first file up anew,
     To seek and find a floorplan showing
     All Castle Sternendach and grounds.
     Right there: the eastern wing surrounds
     A library. The papers stowing,
     She hunts the office for a pen
     And paper as the clock strikes ten.

15. She scraps the first draft of her letter,
     Its eager scribblings fit to shred.
     The second version fares no better,
     So formal it can scarce be read.
     Here Kunigunde takes a breather,
     At this point satisfied with neither
     Her courage nor her skill. At length,
     The tales of heroes give her strength,
     And she begins once more to shape her
     Request in writing. Soon the lines
     Come easily. She stops and signs
     The bottom, neatly folds the paper,
     Then slips out silent as a ghost
     To put her letter in the post.

16. The next two days seem never-ending.
    As Kinge plays the waiting game,
    She kills the dragging time by spending
    It practicing her draw and aim
    Down at the range, and then reviewing
    Her Latin verbs, perhaps renewing
    Her interest in some other chore,
    Like sweeping out the weapons store.
    On Sunday, still no satisfaction.
    She goes to mass with Eva, takes
    Some lunch with her as well, then breaks
    For home, alone. In her distraction,
    She almost misses, in the door,
    The very thing she's waiting for.

17. A square of paper, neatly folded,
    And sealed with a familiar crest,
    But Kinge trembles as if scolded
    To see the envelope's addressed
    To her. She breaks the waxen sealing.
    The paper parts at once, revealing
    A text that's typed and, scrawled below,
    A signature she doesn't know.
    "Dear Fraülein, greetings, your request to
    Consult the Castle's library
    Is granted by His Exc'llency
    For Monday night. It would be best you
    Present yourself here right at eight.
    You'll have two hours. Don't be late."

18. By Monday night, she's lost in heady
    Anticipation. She secures
    The book inside a satchel, ready
    For deep discussion. She procures
    A taxi, feels herself the essence
    Of grown-up, 'til she's in the presence
    Of Timoch, and that mood deflates.
    She summons up some hauteur, states:
    "Good ev'ning, Timoch. I'm expected."
    He answers: "Nice to see you back.
    I fear, though, you must leave your pack.
    The Graf's desires will be respected."
    "But how can I…?" she starts to plead.
    "I'll bring you anything you need."

19. The library is warm, inviting.
    Wood carvings decorate the wall.
    And from gas chandeliers, the lighting
    With golden tones suffuses all.
    Arranged in stacks, the book collections
    Extend to ells in both directions,
    While volumes by the hundreds squeeze
    In alcoves and in balconies.
    To Kunigunde, Timoch carries
    A sheaf of paper, pencils too,
    And turns to leave, as if on cue.
    "But will the Graf be here?" she queries.
    It isn't clear that Timoch hears.
    "Two hours." Then he disappears.

20. Thus Kunigunde, her heart racing,
    Has found herself, alone at last,
    'Mid books and maps and volumes tracing
    The castle's dark and storied past.
    A wealth of knowledge, close and tempting,
    And yet the chamber seems quite empty.
    No sound, no shadow, breath or ghost
    Of her mysterious ancient host
    To greet her as she wanders, shyly
    Exploring stacks and brushing spines.
    So thwarted in her search for signs,
    "I guess I'll read," she whispers wryly.
    She settles in a cozy nook
    And greets a heavy, pond'rous book.

21. The balconies are hiding places
    That Kunigund' does not discern.
    On one of them the vampire paces
    And listens to the pages turn.
    Why is she here? What inspiration
    Has made her seek his invitation?
    He peers down at his guest below
    And wonders: does Luzia know?
    Her grandmother would have prevented
    The girl from seeing him alone,
    And burned the letter, had she known.
    He grasps, perhaps, what made her send it.
    For surely one as old as he
    Knows books aren't what she came to see.

22. Two hours pass and, disappointed,
    She leaves the books in piles about.
    When Timoch shows up, as appointed,
    She sighs and lets him walk her out.
    Once home, she snubs her mother's greeting
    And, quickly to her room retreating,
    She shuts the door and turns the key.
    Oh God, how stupid could she be?
    Of course he wouldn't deign to see her,
    Or answer to her naïve call,
    If he was even home at all!
    To make it worse, well, what if he were
    To tell her fam'ly where she'd been?
    Her grandmother would do her in!

23. Embarrassment and worry racking
    Her nerves, she drops down on the bed
    And grabs her bag to start unpacking—
    But finds an envelope instead.
    His crest again but, more exciting,
    The letter's in his handsome writing:
    "*Geehrtes* Fräulein, pleased was I
    My library should catch your eye.
    I could not join you, to my sorrow.
    Two hours is not ample time
    For large collections such as mine.
    Would you return at eight tomorrow?
    Then you will have, you may be sure,
    My presence, and a proper tour."

24. She's thunderstruck. Of course, she's going.
    But writing her like this implies
    He wants to see her. Her! And knowing
    This fact, some questions soon arise,
    Like, this time, how will Timoch greet her?
    How quickly will his master meet her?
    And once met, will they be alone?
    What clothes would set the proper tone?
    The Tuesday ev'ning finds she chose her
    Green dress again, with Eva's shoes.
    On her arrival, Timoch, whose
    Demeanor is unaltered, shows her
    To where his lord waits patiently
    To show the guest his library.

25. The brass doors part at Timoch's knocking.
    "Come in, please," says a voice within.
    His voice. That *voice*. She leans back, rocking
    A little as the sound sinks in,
    Eyes closed. But stop! The Graf is waiting!
    She shakes her head clear, concentrating,
    And holds her head up high, before
    She steps past Timoch, through the door.
    The Graf looks up and puts the book he
    Was reading quickly to the side.
    Before her in a single stride,
    And wearing a most genial look, he
    Says, "Ah, you're here. You cannot guess
    How glad I am that you've said yes."

26.   The Graf extends his hand. She takes it.
      He says, "I've chosen to surround
      Myself with precious things, which makes it
      My honor, showing you around."
      "The honor's mine," she says, and follows
      Him through the chamber's aisles and hollows.
      She seems calm, but inside? A storm.
      Oh, Oma lies. His hand is warm.
      The books are treasures, vast, uncounted.
      He draws her deeper in, to show
      The works he has in folio
      By Plutarch and by Kircher. Mounted
      In frames above are pages ripped
      From some Tchaikovsky manuscript.

27.   He speaks with such enthusiasm
      She cannot help but be drawn in.
      For every item, Kinge has him
      Describe its import, origin,
      And he indulges her. Attentive
      She nonetheless finds fair incentive
      To study how he speaks and moves
      Up close, in detail. "If this proves
      A bore," he says, "Too desultory…?"
      "It's part of you," she says, "I see
      Why you keep them so carefully.
      Each book you have contains a story,
      Inside and out, a mem'ry fit
      To last forever." "Yes. That's it."

28. A glass case in a further section
    Displays a codex, old and faint:
    A treatise on the Resurrection
    By Isentrud, the local saint.
    This item Kinge finds amazing.
    She stands before the showcase, gazing.
    Then, feeling just a little proud,
    She reads some Latin text aloud,
    And praises the illumination.
    Her words trail off into the air
    When she perceives the vampire's stare.
    His eyes are hard. A cold sensation
    Creeps up her arms. His face austere,
    He asks, "What are you doing here?"

29. She, startled, asks, "Did I offend you?"
    He waves her silent with his hand.
    "Just tell me. Did Luzia send you?
    What sort of mischief has she planned?"
    "She doesn't know I'm here, I swear. She's
    In Serbia." "Yes, I'm aware. She's
    Been gone a week, but even so,
    There's little that she doesn't know."
    The path behind her—Timoch's blocked it,
    Discreetly moving into view,
    And trapping her between the two.
    The Graf says, "Seeing you've concocted
    This scheme to meet me, tell me why.
    Believe I'll know it if you lie."

30. His accusation stings, afflicting
    The girl with unexpected dread.
    She spies a canvas then, depicting
    The old Graf, Syfryd, who is dead
    By Heller hands, and realizes
    The image of her in his eyes is
    An enemy, a fam'ly curse.
    Well might it seem to him perverse
    That she should risk so much in senseless
    Pursuit of his attention. Could
    She melt away right now, she would.
    But here she is, pinned and defenseless,
    And praying for some sign of ruth.
    What can she tell him, but the truth?

31. "Do you remember our first meeting,
    When you gave me that book?" "What book?"
    He interrupts, and it's defeating,
    The lack of knowledge in his look.
    "*The Stars of Sternendach*, the fairy
    And wonder tales," she says. "With very
    Detailed designs that caught the light?"
    "Ah, yes." "I read it every night,"
    She presses on. "Before I met you
    My Oma told me to prepare
    For someone cold, who didn't care
    For anything but blood. And yet you
    Gave me a host of magic friends
    Whose brav'ry earned them happy ends.

32. "I grew up, spent the last years vowing
    That childish things and I were through.
    But when I saw you Friday, bowing,
    I wanted magic. Wanted you."
    Her courage gone, she reaches blindly
    For some support, which Timoch kindly
    Provides by bringing her a chair.
    She sits and gulps much-needed air.
    The Graf's not even looking at her,
    His focus on his father's face,
    Then on the codex in its case.
    She grits her teeth to stop their chatter.
    Her hands' heels pressed against her eyes,
    She holds the tears back. Well, she tries.

33. Warm hands on hers her face uncover,
    Keen eyes on hers rest for a beat.
    She blinks, bewildered, to discover
    Her host is kneeling at her feet.
    "Forgive me," he says, "I implore you.
    One woman only, once before you,
    Has ever sought me out, and she
    Was hardly moved by love for me."
    Releasing her, he rises, saying,
    "You're free to leave, if you prefer."
    So pensive does he look to her,
    She softly asks, "And if I'm staying?"
    He says, "Then, Fräulein, ere you go,
    There's one more thing I have to show.

34. "But first, I think, you will be needing
    A lantern." This he finds, and lights.
    He gestures her to follow, leading
    Her through a door. "It's several flights,"
    He says. And there, illumined gently,
    A spiral stair. She peers intently,
    But lantern light can't reach the top.
    "Go on. I'll tell you when to stop,"
    He says, and at her hesitation
    The Graf stands back, to make it clear
    That she is not a captive here.
    No trap. No Timoch. Invitation.
    She takes the light and starts to climb
    The cool stone steps, one at a time.

35. A spiral staircase never varies.
    It's steps above and steps below,
    Pitch black but for the light she carries,
    No way to tell how far to go.
    She hears her ragged breath escaping,
    Her shoes against the granite scraping,
    And wonders if she's like to fall.
    His footsteps make no sound at all.
    Nor has he spoken. It's confounding.
    She'd turn, but cannot shake the fear
    That if she did, he'd disappear.
    She freezes. Then his voice comes, sounding
    So close she feels it on her hair.
    "Don't give up now; you're almost there."

36. Just five more steps, then Kinge faces
    A doorway open to the night.
    Beyond, a parapet that places
    Her at the castle's greatest height.
    The views between the merlons show her
    The city, sparkling far below her,
    Stray lights like grains of gold on black.
    But color draws her eyeline back
    And up, where swaths of blue and violet
    Play host to stars of every size
    And brightness. "Oh, my God!" she cries,
    Enthralled. She's never seen the sky lit
    Up quite like this. She starts to spin,
    Arms out, to take the splendor in.

37. Her soul awash with starlight, soaring,
    She doesn't see the roughness where
    Her high heel catches on the flooring,
    And Kinge's fingers close on air
    As she spills backwards t'ward the paving.
    He swoops in like a kestrel, saving
    Her dizzy form from falling. Through
    His grace, he saves the lantern, too.
    He murmurs, "Oh, how you enchant me."
    She's waiting for their lips to meet,
    But he returns her to her feet.
    "Why not?" the girl demands. "Why can't we?"
    He looks at her. "Because, my lamb,
    Of who you are. And who I am."

38. "Oh yes," she says, "I've known who you are
    My whole life, just like you've known me."
    "And from that, you believe we two are…?"
    "We have no secrets here. We're free."
    He laughs, but there's no malice in it.
    Completely silent for a minute,
    When next he speaks, it's tinged with rue.
    "I think I am too old for you."
    "For everyone," she says, "I grant you.
    Four hundred years." He frowns. "Quite so."
    His eyes reflect the heavens' glow.
    She asks, a whisper, "I enchant you?"
    The stars and castle crash and blur
    As he leans in and kisses her.

39. Once home, and calm, she risks believing
    She dreamed the stair, the stars, the kiss.
    But then must she deny receiving
    His invitation back, and this
    She will not do. Thus start recurring
    Excursions to the castle. During
    The next few weeks the vampire looks
    For her each night among his books,
    Where Kunigunde gladly tarries.
    They read each other soft refrains
    Of poetry the times it rains,
    But when the weather's clear, he carries
    Her up the spiral stair and they
    Embrace beneath the sky's display.

40. One morning, Kinge's mother tasks her
    With setting out their breakfast of
    Fresh bread and honey. Kinge asks her,
    "When did you know you were in love?"
    Here Eva eyes her daughter wisely.
    "With Papa?" she asks, smiles. "Precisely?
    First time I saw that gorgeous man.
    In uniform, no less. You can
    Imagine, he cut such a figure."
    Now Kinge pouts and rolls her eyes.
    "That isn't love, you know," she sighs.
    Says Eva, "Are you now so big, you're
    About to teach me what love means,
    With all the wisdom of your teens?"

41. She sips her tea. "All right, that part was
    Admittedly a bit cliché.
    But nonetheless, it's true: my heart was
    Completely lost to him that day.
    And very quickly I would know that
    He was a hero, fighting so that
    He'd save some lives, help end the war.
    But that's not what you're asking for."
    A pause. "Your Father took me dancing
    In Syfryd Park, some summer night.
    He held me in his arms so tight,
    With starlight all around us glancing,
    As if the world were just us two.
    And that, my dear, was when I knew.

42. "I didn't know how complicated
    His life was. I knew he loved me,
    But not how much his mother hated
    His choice. She said I'd never be
    A hunter, calling me 'outsider.'"
    And Eva's dark eyes flash. Beside her,
    Her daughter comes to sit. "So do
    I look like him, or more like you?"
    Her mother tells her, with affection,
    "I see him in you, here and there.
    You've got his nose, and that's his hair.
    But you've my eyes, and my complexion."
    The girl beams proudly, taking in
    Her mother's lovely olive skin.

43. There's silence in the air between them
    As Kunigunde starts to clear
    Their breakfast things away to clean them.
    Says Eva, "Something you should hear:
    When you were born, your father planned to
    Take both of us and leave this land, to
    Start over somewhere, maybe France.
    I'm mad we never got the chance."
    Her daughter nearly drops a plate, her
    Mouth open. "But, the pact!" she cries.
    "The vampires!" Eva then replies,
    "D'you think the world holds dangers greater
    Than vampires who've sworn not to kill?
    Your father did; I hope you will.

44. "Your grandmother will not accept that.
    She thinks she's right, and we should sign
    Ourselves to her crusade, except that
    Her son refused to fall in line."
    "So Papa quit," says Kunigunde,
    "He joined the army." "Which served under
    The Graf's direct authority.
    They fought about it constantly.
    One night they wouldn't stop their yelling.
    Your Opa tried to calm him down.
    They took a car ride into town
    And then..." Now Eva's eyes are welling.
    The girl approaches, gingerly.
    "Let's talk 'bout something else," says she.

45. "But thanks," she adds, "for what you told me,"
    Though she's not sure she understood.
    "Your Oma isn't here to scold me.
    I had to tell you, while I could,"
    Says Eva, dries her eyes. "I'm guessing
    There is a reason you're obsessing
    About the mail, and going in
    To town." A blush warms Kinge's skin.
    Has Mama found her out? She couldn't!
    And when she's asked, "Is it a boy?"
    She blushes deeper. "Well, enjoy!"
    Her mother laughs. "I'm sure you wouldn't
    Do anything I wouldn't do."
    "I love you, Mama." "Love you, too."

46. Her mother's tale and gloomy meaning
    Disquiet Kunigunde, true.
    But she can't help her mind careening
    To thoughts of her next rendez-vous.
    One detail, though, her conscience bothers:
    The medal that she found—her father's—
    Is locked away from prying eyes.
    Should she tell Eva where it lies?
    But that would lead to more discussions
    Of her nocturnal research, so
    She thinks it best to let it go
    For now, and chance the repercussions.
    For what means all of that beside
    A castle with her love inside?

Complications

1. Now, living in the vampire's castle,
    And watching some of this unfold,
    Is Sternendach's one human vassal,
    Named Galen. Forty-five years old,
    For half his life has he been serving
    His undead master's will, observing
    The daylight world on his behalf
    And managing the castle staff.
    He has his secret tasks, like stocking
    The cellars full of blood and wine,
    Should Graf or guests desire to dine.
    When night time comes, it finds him clocking
    More hours as he's occupied
    With matters on the distaff side.

2.   Although the Graf's noblesse induced him
     To faithful service from the start,
     It was the Gräfin first seduced him,
     And she's the one who holds his heart.
     About now she should be returning.
     He pictures her, with new blood burning,
     Alive like no one else he's known,
     And heading to her room alone.
     Her perfume hanging in the hallways—
     A blend of honey, cloves, and myrrh—
     Compels him, draws him near to her.
     She's waiting for him, just like always.
     Her smile is fire, her teeth are keen,
     And he relates the things he's seen.

3.   "Our lord, your husband's, had a visit.
     One Kunigunde Heller's been…"
     "A Heller? Oh my God, then is it
     Already time to bring her in?"
     "They talk about his books for hours,"
     Says Galen, while his mistress glowers,
     "Just sitting in the library."
     She sniffs. "Well, better her than me.
     And yet," Amata says, "It's funny,
     Him cozy with the Heller spawn.
     Why don't you learn what's going on?"
     "Just how, pray tell? I'm not the one he
     Would tell his secrets to." "You're right.
     The Graf would not; the girl just might."

4. The girl, to nobody's surprise, is
    Among the stacks and racks and stands.
    In cotton gloves, she scrutinizes
    The priceless codex in her hands.
    The Graf observes her careful motions,
    Engaging her insightful notions.
    She asks him, as she pages through,
    "How did this volume come to you?"
    "From Isentrud," he says, "My sister.
    My human sister. Long ago."
    This startles her. "I didn't know
    That you had fam'ly. Do you miss her?"
    Asks Kinge, feigning nonchalance.
    "When I remember," his response.

5. She turns a page, but her attention
    Has wandered and will not return.
    His sister? Just the passing mention
    Reminds her she has much to learn.
    She holds the codex out, and gently
    He takes it from her, reverently
    Replacing it within its case.
    This should be just the time and place
    For questions she would ask, addressing
    His other fam'ly, former loves…
    But slowly he pulls off her gloves
    And with her hands in his, starts pressing
    A line of kisses 'cross her palms
    Which any question soon becalms.

6.   An ornate mantel clock is chiming.
      She shuts her eyes and counts the tones.
      Eleven! Oh, what awful timing!
      "It's late. I have to go," she groans.
      Another kiss, as soft and thrilling.
      He asks, "Tomorrow? If you're willing."
      "I am. 'Til then, Your Exc'llency."
      He winces, just perceptibly.
      And she thought she'd run out of blushes.
      A little smile, he draws her near
      And whispers, "Georg," in her ear.
      As he draws back, he lightly brushes
      A finely wrought and sparkling strand
      Of silver chain into her hand.

7.   She lifts the chain before her, letting
      Its length play out in graceful lines.
      Appended in a simple setting
      A flawless gemstone softly shines.
      He says, "This is a tiny treasure,
      But I thought one who shares my pleasure
      In gazing at the starry dome
      Might like a star she may take home."
      There's silence. "Though, you needn't wear it.
      It's old; perhaps it's not your style."
      But Kinge still says nothing while
      She hangs it 'round her neck, and there it
      Sits glist'ning, rivalling the skies.
      "It's perfect, Georg," she replies.

8.   Outside the library, she's waiting
For Timoch, who has yet to show,
When Kunigund' hears someone stating,
"You're out late, kid. Does Mother know?"
She flusters. "Galen, don't surprise me!"
"It's like you didn't recognize me,"
Says Galen. "Oh, of course I did,"
She says, "And please don't call me 'kid.'"
Whenever Galen speaks, affecting
His roguish air, she plays along.
She hasn't known him very long,
But cannot help herself correcting
His harmless shots. "She knows I'm out.
It's nothing she's concerned about."

9.   He grins. "Forgive my rude suggestions."
She does, and almost instantly,
Because she has so many questions
She wants to ask, if only she
Could find the nerve. "This may be prying,"
He says, "I heard the Graf implying
That Oma's coming back next week."
And Kinge finds she cannot speak.
"That's rough," says Galen, "She is scary.
But look, your secret's safe with me."
He leans in confidentially.
"I know this isn't customary,
But I can drive you home tonight.
It's faster than a cab." "All right."

10. He glances in the rearview mirror
    At Kinge's lost and dreamy stare.
    She's lovestruck; that could not be clearer.
    He'd know that half-smile anywhere.
    He used to wear it. But this mission
    Will take much more than intuition.
    "You're quite the little bookworm, you,"
    He says, "What is it draws you to
    Those dusty things?" "They're fascinating,"
    She answers, "Each one forms a link
    To people—souls—long gone. I think
    Just holding them's exhilarating."
    He snickers at this florid hymn.
    "Does that describe the books, or him?"

11. The nerve is touched, he sees, and nicely.
    "You love him," he says, "That, I get."
    "My Oma said you're…" "What, precisely?"
    "She says that you're the Gräfin's…" "Pet?"
    She meekly cringes once he's said it,
    Which means he's right. He says, "Forget it.
    She's called me worse. She doesn't know
    What being with them feels like, though."
    He checks the mirror, seeing whether
    She's felt that electricity.
    She rubs her palms distractedly.
    "How long have you two been together?"
    She asks. He shifts to overdrive.
    "For longer than you've been alive."

12. She inches closer, slowly, questing,
    Until she leans upon the seat
    Beside his. Chin on fingers resting,
    She asks him, "How did you two meet?"
    Not hiding wicked glee, he chortles,
    "The same way she meets many mortals."
    It takes a second, then an "Oh..."
    Slips, awkward, from her lips. And so
    It's safe to say she's not been bitten.
    "If you could know the mess I was,"
    He tells her. "I'm alive because
    She saved me. I was young then, smitten
    With her. Who wouldn't be? God knows,
    I'm lucky I'm the one she chose."

13. He bites the last word off. Now why did
    He tell her all of that? And will
    It even work, as some misguided
    Attempt to get the girl to spill?
    She's silent, then, "Has Georg ever...?"
    "Stop. *Georg?*" Galen blurts. "I've never
    Heard even Timoch call him that."
    "He told me to," she answers, flat.
    There's something in this information
    That bothers him; he can't tell what.
    He feels like he should warn her, but
    They come upon their destination
    And Kinge gasps as they arrive.
    "That's Oma's car parked in the drive."

14. So Galen taps the gas and glides them
    Beyond the drive and over to
    A little copse of trees, which hides them
    Away from any Heller view.
    They sit there, with the engine humming.
    Says Kunigund', "She wasn't coming
    Back home 'til Friday. I don't know
    What's happening, but you should go.
    Please tell…" She swallows, looking sickly.
    "The Graf… I can't… tomorrow night…"
    "I'll tell him. It'll be all right,"
    Says Galen. "Now go home, and quickly."
    With mumbled thanks she's out the door.
    He puts the pedal to the floor.

15. The car gone, Kinge stands regretting
    She can't go, too. She starts the trek
    Toward her house, almost forgetting
    To slip the pendant off her neck.
    Once in, the rasp of conversation
    Floats from the kitchen. There's temptation
    To duck upstairs, avoid a row.
    No, better have it over now.
    Like breadcrumbs, Kinge follows snatches
    Of sound which louden bit by bit.
    Her mother and Luzia sit
    Discussing her, from what she catches
    Until the latter notices.
    Luzia smiles. "Well, there she is."

16. The girl sees many things amiss here.
     She must keep Oma off the scent.
     "So how was Kisilova this year?"
     Luzia answers, "Different.
     Old Stepan quit, if you believe it.
     Their finest hunter! Chose to leave it
     To Luka, have him run the show.
     My God, they're all so soft and slow."
     She downs the kirsch that Eva pours her.
     "At least their vampires are so few
     That Luka's meager hunts should do."
     She yawns, as though the subject bores her.
     "I'm home now, and you both look stunned.
     So where have you been, Kunigund'?"

17. The girl blinks back and swallows tightly,
     While Eva pours herself a glass.
     "The library," says Kinge, lightly.
     It's not a lie, and might just pass
     For truth. Luzia's gaze is steely.
     "The library, near midnight? Really?
     I thought they were on summer break."
     But Eva snaps, "For heaven's sake,
     She finally made some friends. So why're
     You giving her the third degree?"
     It troubles Kunigund' to see
     Her mother turned unwitting liar.
     She'll take the lifeline anyway.
     "I'm off to bed, if that's okay."

18. She leaves the two alone to bicker
    (Time later for apology)
    But envies them at least the liquor;
    A drop or two for her would be
    Most welcome. Her room's dark and lonely.
    She sits and sighs and wishes only
    To get a message to the Graf
    With no clue how to pull it off.
    There's pen and paper; she could write it.
    But mailing it might prove too hard,
    With Oma always on her guard.
    His number he has not provided,
    And does an ancient vampire own,
    Or know to use, a telephone?

19. Her palms still tingle where he kissed her;
    It sends a thrumming to her core.
    Delicious. Oh, but has she missed her
    One chance of ever knowing more?
    It hurts, just now, this separation.
    Her eyes sting, and in desperation
    She crosses to her window, throws
    It open, leaning out. Suppose
    She could but see the castle during
    This exile, it might seem less long,
    Except the house is angled wrong.
    The stars would likewise be assuring.
    She'd watch them, but by rotten chance
    The heavy clouds obscure their dance.

20. While Kunigund' the weather curses,
    Her erstwhile driver takes the streets
    Too fast, and in his mind rehearses
    Just what he'll say when next he meets
    His lady. Could be a disaster.
    But first things first. He finds his master
    Within his study, drinking up
    Red blood from out a silver cup.
    The Graf reveals but scant emotion
    As he receives the girl's regrets.
    And if the other news upsets
    Him further, Galen has no notion.
    To press would be to overplay
    And give his lady's game away.

21. Dismissed, but with a brief reminder
    To check the larder, Galen seeks
    The Gräfin, knowing he will find her
    In his room, as they planned. She speaks:
    "You're back, my love. With news, I gather.
    So will you tell, or would you rather
    I guess?" He pauses, breathing in
    The sultry perfume from her skin.
    "The girl is quite infatuated,"
    Says Galen. "Has that moony air.
    She does like books, though, to be fair."
    "And is this crush reciprocated?"
    The Gräfin asks, a touch too fast,
    And Galen looks at her, aghast.

22. "My lady, are you jealous of her?
    A goddess, and you fear the worst!
    I'm sure the Graf has had his lovers."
    "Oh, no," she tells him. "She's the first.
    The first since he and I were married,
    The first since he the old Graf buried.
    For decades, books are all he sees.
    So answer me my question! Please."
    Bewildered by this, Galen mutters,
    "The hell should I know? Honestly,
    The girl said no such thing to me."
    Except, he thinks but never utters,
    There is one fact belies this claim:
    The Graf gave Kunigund' his name.

23. He's never seen his lady shiver,
    Nor any kind of worry show.
    He thinks what comfort he may give her
    And pulls her close. "Here's what I know:
    Whatever those two have, it's over,
    Or will be soon, 'cause when I drove her
    Back home tonight she got a scare.
    It seems Luzia beat us there."
    "Luzia's back?" "The one and only,"
    Says Galen, nodding, "who, no doubt,
    Would kill them if she caught them out.
    So Kinge will resume her lonely
    Existence under Oma's thumb,
    Perhaps from now 'til kingdom come."

24. He waits for her to call his bluff, then
    Her mouth finds his. Her lips are cold.
    The feed before was not enough, then,
    Her thirst not sated, just controlled.
    Well, that makes anybody testy.
    He laughs a bit, but softly, lest he
    Lead her, mistakenly, to feel
    That her thirst holds him no appeal.
    "I missed you," whispers Galen, "Driving
    That silly human girl around—
    Your eyes, your skin, and most, the sound
    Of my name on your tongue. Depriving
    Me so was cruel, and I'd be sore
    But you, dear Amy, missed me more."

25. He kisses her this time, just teasing
    Her lips and teeth, then pulls away.
    "Oh, Galen," says the Gräfin, seizing
    Him by the waist, "In ev'ry way."
    Strong arms enfold him, pressing, pinning.
    He sighs at tingling warmth beginning
    Beneath her kiss, which dulls the pain
    When fang teeth pierce a favorite vein:
    This time, a soft spot on his shoulder.
    He's not quite numb, but doesn't care.
    Enveloped in her scent and hair,
    He brings his arms around to hold her
    And breathes her name again. He sinks
    Unconscious as the vampire drinks.

26.   When Galen finally wakens, first he
      Turns on the dim light by his bed.
      His head throbs and, good God, he's thirsty!
      But by the lamp, a plate of bread,
      Fresh fruit and meat in equal measure,
      And sparkling water wait his pleasure.
      She's always so considerate,
      But when did she deliver it?
      He eats and thinks. It's kind to feed him,
      And normally he can't complain.
      But feeding her is such a drain.
      Whatever. Castle duties need him.
      It's time to put the food away,
      Unseal the curtains, greet the day.

27.   A pretzel in his mouth, he braces
      Himself for morning's glaring light.
      Instead he pulls the drapes and faces
      The darkness of another night.
      He checks his watch. Has he been lying
      Abed for nineteen hours? Spying
      And intrigue—not his kind of fun.
      It wears him out; he's glad it's done.
      Course now, he's running late. He duly
      Throws on some clothing, smooths his hair,
      Steps out into the hall. And there
      Stands Timoch, who regards him coolly,
      Then says, "Awake and ready? You've
      Been summoned to the study. Move."

28. The study's air is close, and smells of
    Old candle smoke and…is that ink?
    A pile of scribbled paper tells of
    A vampire with too much to think.
    The Graf sits in his desk chair, brooding.
    Asks Galen, "Sire, am I intruding?"
    His lord examines him a spell.
    "Of course not, Galen. Slept you well?"
    Embarrassed, Galen says, "You needed
    Me at my work, I know, and I'm
    Afraid that I lost track of time.
    I'm sorry. It won't be repeated."
    The Graf remarks, "Perhaps it should.
    More rest, I think, might do you good."

29. Might do us both, is Galen's thinking.
    He finds amid the paper pile
    The cup from which the Graf was drinking.
    It's empty; has been for a while.
    That would explain his master's ashen
    Complexion. Galen, with compassion,
    Asks, "Were you up all day, my lord?
    And have you fed?" But he's ignored.
    The Graf says, "Kunigunde Heller
    Attends St. Paul's at eight-fifteen.
    Take her this letter. Don't be seen."
    But Galen asks, "What does it tell her?"
    The vampire's eyes are sharp and stern.
    "Is any of that your concern?"

30. The question's fair, and though it greatly
    Unnerves him, he may not demur.
    "It's not at all, my lord. But lately
    I find myself concerned for her."
    The Graf sits back, the letter resting
    Between his fingers. "Interesting,"
    He says, his face a marble mask.
    "Where is my wife, if I may ask?"
    "Don't know. I have no plans to see her,"
    Says Galen. "Too much work to do:
    Buy blood, deliver this for you…
    Tomorrow night I may be freer."
    The Graf hands him the folded square.
    "Then do get to it, and take care."

31. He takes the note and his assignment—
    His headache, too, which grows more grim—
    And leaves the Graf to his confinement
    While Timoch, quiet, watches him.
    At any given moment, it is
    Unclear just how much Timoch, in his
    Cool silence, knows of anything.
    A wise man figures: everything.
    When Timoch says, "She's looking for you,"
    No points for guessing who is "she."
    Sighs Galen, "Know where she might be?"
    A shrug. "She was upstairs, before you
    Emerged. But now…?" "All right, all right.
    Just…please make sure he feeds tonight."

32. She's sulking on a sofa when he
Arrives in the salon at last.
He says, "If I had wanted any
More vampire moping, I'd have passed
My ev'ning in the Graf's location.
Or Timoch's, for the conversation."
She scowls. "Do watch your tone," says she.
"I can't. My head is killing me."
She rolls her lovely eyes, but beckons
The man to join her sitting there.
Her fingers sinking in his hair
Massage his scalp. In only seconds
Her cool and graceful fingers take
The edge away and soothe the ache.

33. He pulls the letter from his jacket.
"This far will he in me confide:
To bring her this." She eyes the packet
Like there's a scorpion inside.
"So you were wrong. They haven't broken."
"We don't know that," he says, "This token
May sing of love that will not die
Or, just as likely, say goodbye."
She's not impressed with his acumen,
It seems. She says, "We'll stop this, yet."
"Oh, leave it, Lady. She's no threat,"
He says. "She's just a kid, a human
Who'll lose whatever charm she's got."
She asks, "And what if she were not?"

34. Her meaning's clear. In agitation,
     He sits up. "But I thought he swore,
     As part of that negotiation,
     That he would not make any more
     Immortals. Hellers won't permit it."
     "The Hellers," she says, "Can't forbid it.
     Their precious pact, in black and white,
     Explicitly gives him the right
     To make more as he likes, provided
     Our total number stay below
     A certain line. And years ago,
     His vassal, Justin, suicided.
     That fief stands empty still, and thus
     There's room for yet one more of us."

35. "All right," he says, not disagreeing,
     "The Graf could, but, you realize,
     He's never turned a human being.
     Why would he now?" "Enough!" she cries,
     And grabs his arm. Her fingers tremble.
     "I know you, Galen. You dissemble.
     There's something you've been holding back.
     He loves her. Isn't that a fact?"
     His arm hurts. "Lady, you are clever,"
     He says. "And it offends your pride
     That he may soon put you aside.
     But would that be the worst thing ever?
     You don't love him. You're not his thrall.
     Why did you marry him at all?"

36. At first, no answer does she tender,
    But then she says, "To play a role.
    A role which I will not surrender.
    I think it's time I took control."
    She drops his arm. "Give me the letter."
    He looks away. "Now, you know better
    Than that. I can't." She nods at this,
    And plants upon his cheek a kiss.
    "I know, my dear. I think this matter
    Requires another sort of guile."
    And wearing a carnassial smile,
    She rises. Galen marvels at her
    In silence as she leaves the room,
    The air hung with her myrrh perfume.

37. The letter. There can be no doubt it
    Was stupid, showing that to her.
    But Galen, now he thinks about it,
    Made his mistake much earlier.
    There's nothing for it now, he knows it,
    But keep the letter safe. He stows it
    Inside his jacket, heaves a sigh.
    Now, doesn't he have blood to buy?
    For that, the night is unproductive
    As one by one, his contacts all
    Are out, or fail to take his call.
    The city's life proves more seductive
    In any case. He finds he's drawn
    To walk its busy streets 'til dawn.

38. This was his city as a younger
    And, doubtless, a more foolish man,
    The site of ev'ry joy and hunger,
    Each deep regret or brilliant plan.
    And like a well-loved coat, it fit him.
    There's comfort in these streets. It hits him
    That though his life's no longer here,
    His youth's haunts did not disappear,
    As if they waited for him. Flattered
    By Time's apparent kindness, he
    Makes fleeting stops at two or three.
    But old coats can be tight, or tattered,
    And he's outgrown his old life, too.
    Is there a chance for something new?

39. The dawn turns dreary, demonstrating
    A bluster more akin to Fall's.
    It buffets Galen as he's waiting
    Outside the narthex of St. Paul's.
    The music starts as mass is ending,
    And soon the congregation, wending
    Its way past Galen, down the stair,
    Begins to scatter to the air.
    Ah, there's Luzia. Watch her scurry
    To snag the priest in some debate.
    There's Eva right behind her. Great,
    That buys him time. Still, Kinge, hurry!
    She comes out. He moves quickly when
    He sees her, taps her shoulder, then

40. Slips back into the church, not slowing
    Until he's at the left-most aisle.
    Then Kinge enters, wide-eyed, glowing
    From candles and a lovely smile
    That warms his heart like breath on embers.
    But then, of course, the man remembers
    It's not for him, but for the one
    Who sent him. "Right, let's get this done,"
    He says aloud as she approaches.
    "For you, from him. Now, need I say
    I wasn't here, and cannot stay?"
    She takes the note, but his reproach is
    Unheard, for as he turns to leave,
    Her hand darts out and grips his sleeve.

41. "Is he all right?" she whispers, pleading.
    "What did he say? What's this about?"
    He pulls his sleeve free. "You like reading.
    You have the letter. Go find out."
    "Wait, Galen. Tell the Graf that after…"
    He stops her with a bark of laughter,
    "I don't know what you think you've seen,
    But I am not your go-between."
    She steps back, speechless, warm glow faded.
    He takes a shot at being nice.
    "It's delicate right now. Advice?
    I'm hoping you can be persuaded
    To stay away from him—for now,"
    He adds as worry marks her brow.

42.   He says, "I know Luzia thwarted
     Your plans. But school starts soon, and if
     You take some time to get that sorted…"
     "That could be weeks!" "I think you'll live,"
     He deadpans. "Which reminds me. You should
     Keep distance from the Gräfin, too, should
     You prize your safety." She asks, "Why?"
     "Oh, why d'you think? Be smart. Goodbye."
     With nothing else, he turns to leave her,
     The letter safely in her hand.
     He thinks she looks so thoughtful and
     So sad. The note may yet relieve her.
     A crying shame he can't do more.
     He exits through the transept door.

43.   The girl resists the urge to open
     The missive; now is not ideal.
     She places all her love and hope in
     The kiss she presses on its seal,
     Then slips it in her purse discreetly.
     She'll read it when she's next completely
     Alone, tonight. That's if she's strong
     Enough inside to wait so long.
     Outside, with their palaver finished,
     Luzia, smug, farewells the priest.
     He seems quite glad to be released,
     Though maybe just a tad diminished
     In dignity as he repairs
     Past Kunigunde up the stairs.

44. She looks from Oma to her mother,
    Who lifts her eyebrows in a shrug.
    They share half-smiles with one another
    Then join together in a hug.
    Conspiracy between these two has
    The past two days begun anew, as
    Luzia's kept them in her sight
    Since her return on Friday night.
    Deep down does Kunigund' suspect that
    While she was out and having fun
    Her mother might the same have done,
    And who is she to disrespect that?
    They ask no questions, which is wise.
    If neither asks, then neither lies.

45. "Please come here, Kinge," calls Luzia.
    The girl, as usual, obeys.
    "Now tell me, sweetheart, do you see the
    Sedan parked up the road a ways?"
    The distance, angle, make it nearly
    Impossible to make out clearly.
    Alas, she knows it even so;
    She rode inside two nights ago.
    "It's Galen's car," says Kinge, keeping
    Her voice low. "Must be here to search
    For us," says Oma, darkly. "Church
    Is not his place. The vampire's sleeping,
    But sent his man our steps to haunt.
    So what does that cold bastard want?"

46. "Don't call him 'cold,'" says Kunigunde.
    She feels a tremor in her jaw
    And hears what might be distant thunder.
    But she stands straight, does not withdraw,
    Nor look for Eva's intercession.
    Luzia, with a dark expression,
    Looks Kunigunde in the eye,
    And says to her, "Why shouldn't I?"
    But Kinge, knowing there's a chance her
    Next words may trap her, merely waits.
    Her Oma scowls. "Go on," she baits.
    Too late. The girl thinks up an answer.
    She says, "I simply think that word
    May sound unfair, if overheard."

47. Luzia says, "Oh, let him hear me.
    The Graf—so dangerous, and yet
    He knows that he has cause to fear me
    And I to hate him. Don't forget,
    Not ever, how the Graf disrupted
    Our fam'ly, first when he corrupted
    My mother, later when he killed
    Her father. Once our blood was spilled,
    He bound us in this fool's arrangement.
    In training you, I've kept you far
    From him, and so I think you are
    Naïve because of that estrangement.
    But I have known the Graf of old,
    And happily I call him 'cold.'"

48. How many times has Kinge heard her
    Repeat this story? Who can say?
    Maria's treachery, the murder,
    Have always seemed so far away.
    But this time, Kinge ponders, silent,
    How both sides in the tale claim violent
    Revenge. She can't tell which is worse.
    Then there's the letter in her purse…
    "So, breakfast?" Eva says, from nowhere.
    She's smiling, as if to defy
    The tension in the air. "Let's try
    The Waldcafe. We never go there."
    "We're going home," says Oma, "You
    Know Kunigund' has chores to do."

49. But Eva only smiles the wider.
    "Luzia, really, I insist.
    Such special meals draw families tighter;
    Once school begins, they will be missed.
    If Galen follows us, we'll lose him.
    We'll take the long way home, confuse him
    With back roads. And I have a hunch
    He doesn't care about our brunch."
    At this, Luzia seems to soften.
    She says, "Then let's get on with it,
    Or they'll have nowhere left to sit."
    Surprising, that. It isn't often
    That Eva wins. They rush to find
    Their car, lest Oma change her mind.

50. The Waldcafe was, sadly, wasted
    On Kinge, who mechanically
    Ate *kaiserschmarrn* but didn't taste it.
    Her mother, grandmother, and she
    Discussed: her start at higher schooling,
    What courses on her list look grueling,
    And how the summer's far too brief—
    Not vampires, to her great relief.
    Now in her room alone, eluding
    Her grandmother, who dogs her more
    Than normal, Kinge locks the door
    Against her possibly intruding.
    She takes a breath to still her heart
    And breaks the letter's seal apart.

51. The first time, she devours the writing
    In one go, at a breathless pace.
    She reads again, more slowly, lighting
    On passages of certain grace.
    A third pass brings her close to weeping.
    She rails against the forces keeping
    Her from his side. She looks again,
    Rememb'ring Oma's stories, then
    She feels a burst of indignation.
    In all this, is she being used?
    By whom? For what? She's so confused.
    The note's no salve for her frustration.
    If she wants answers, she must by
    Herself go seek them where they lie.

Revelations

1. Amata long has been suspicious
   Of märchen told her as a child.
   She noticed early those pernicious
   Untruths they sell to those beguiled,
   So much that even now she winces
   At tales of farm girls wed to princes.
   She sees the irony—she knows
   The ways her life resembles those.
   But bedtime stories oft conflated
   The man you married with the one
   You loved for pleasure and for fun,
   And that's the part she always hated.
   Hell, even in her human day
   She knew things didn't work that way.

2. So when the Graf proposed they marry,
    Romantic love was, from the start,
    Unlikely and unnecessary;
    This was no business of the heart.
    Now as the Gräfin, she possesses
    All that her heart could want—the dresses,
    The title, wealth, security,
    A handsome human devotee.
    The Graf she lends through her indenture
    The gloss of human normalcy,
    Deflecting certain scrutiny
    While Galen she enjoys sans censure.
    A husband and a lover, too:
    The perfect fairy tale come true.

3. Success at years of this endeavor
    Suggests her point of view prevails.
    She knows her husband well, however.
    He has not lost his faith in tales.
    And so it is with trepidation
    She thinks on his new fascination,
    This Kunigunde, knowing she's
    Descended from his enemies.
    Let him bewitch the minds and senses
    Of human girls. Why should she care?
    Nor has she any thought to spare
    For Heller pacts and consequences.
    But his desire for *this* girl spurs
    The Gräfin to protect what's hers.

4. So Sunday, as the Graf is dressing,
   The Gräfin knocks upon his door.
   He stares at her, perhaps assessing
   Whatever she could be here for.
   "To what, my lady, do I owe this
   Rare pleasure?" says the Graf. "I know this
   Intrudes upon your privacy,"
   She says, "But will you speak with me?"
   He lets her pass inside. Unhurried,
   He finds his vest and puts it on.
   "I looked for you last night 'til dawn,"
   She says. "Where did you go? I worried."
   He cocks an eyebrow, says, "Indeed?
   I went with Timoch, out to feed.

5. "What did you want?" Amata planned her
   Next words, but finds them hard to say.
   He says, "I've always liked your candor.
   Don't disappoint me now, I pray."
   She takes a breath. "I ask permission
   To transform Galen. In addition,
   On him that empty fief bestow."
   He thinks for half a second. "No."
   She thought he'd say that. "Do consider
   His years of service here, my lord.
   Such faithfulness deserves reward."
   The Graf's reply is slightly bitter.
   "Believe me, Galen will be paid.
   But that is not the deal we made."

6. From her he turns to face the mirror.
    She tries, "But now, you could arrange..."
    He cuts her off. "Let me be clearer:
    Your lover does not want to change.
    A fact, my lady, I expect you
    Would know unless, as I suspect, you
    Have not asked Galen for his choice."
    She answers in a shaky voice,
    And looks away from his reflection,
    "You don't know him as well as I."
    He carefully adjusts his tie.
    "I know the signs of disaffection
    That he has just begun to show.
    I think it's time we let him go."

7. He slides his jacket off its hanger.
    She says, "You mean to kill him, then?"
    She first mistakes his look for anger,
    And steps back, but is startled when
    He breaks into a peal of laughter
    That shakes the room from floor to rafter.
    "I kill him? With Luzia there
    To take my head if I should dare?
    That's madness. No. A gen'rous pension
    Should keep him quiet once he's gone,
    And not one drop of blood be drawn."
    "Your plan rests on misapprehension,"
    She says. "That man belongs to me.
    He may not go so willingly."

8. She pauses for his answer, wary.
   He shrugs the jacket on, and smooths
   The creases. "He was temporary.
   You knew that then. But if it soothes
   You, know they always are. It's trying."
   He takes her hands and muses, sighing,
   "A shame, my dear, we do not find
   Such feeling here, with our own kind."
   There's truth in that. He has been lenient
   With her, but his years let him be,
   Those hundreds to her seventy.
   She says, "Yes, that would be convenient.
   Our diff'rences are far too vast."
   She pulls back, but he holds her fast.

9. "There's one more thing we must get settled."
   His eyes take on a fearsome shine.
   "In your affair I have not meddled;
   Now cease your meddling in mine."
   Her heart drops like a hammer, shocking
   Her silent. Then they hear a knocking
   And Timoch in the doorway stands,
   The silver goblet in his hands.
   "Forgive me, Sire, for my intrusion,
   But plans have changed, if you'll allow,
   And you will want to drink this now."
   The Graf's brow furrows in confusion.
   Says Timoch, "You have company.
   She's sitting in the library."

10. The Gräfin sees the knowledge breaking
     Upon her husband's face. The Graf's
     Hard grip releases her, and taking
     The cup that Timoch brought, he quaffs
     Its contents. "Timoch, God, she shouldn't..."
     "I know that, Sire, but still, I couldn't
     Just send her off. Or was I wrong?"
     The Graf says, "No." He takes a long
     Look at his fingers, which he touches
     To Timoch's. Says the Graf, "Like ice.
     This cup alone will not suffice."
     Says Timoch, "I gave you as much as
     We have right now. There is no more."
     "But isn't that what Galen's for?"

11. The Graf asks Timoch this, while eyeing
     The Gräfin. Timoch notes his glare
     And measures it before replying,
     "I can't find Galen anywhere."
     His master growls, "Well, that perplexes.
     I'll manage, though." Again he flexes
     His fingers. "Good that you've arrived.
     It seems the Gräfin's been deprived
     Of her companion, and we musn't
     Have that. So would you see that she
     Gets everywhere she needs to be
     Tonight? And nowhere that she doesn't?"
     Here Timoch nods. His smile is slight.
     "With pleasure, Sire. Enjoy your night."

12. Among the books, upon the floor of
    The second-highest balcony,
    Sits Kunigunde, with a store of
    Old letters resting on her knee.
    She'd shown up unannounced, begged entry
    Of Timoch, ever-watchful sentry,
    And he gave in, though she's surprised
    He left her here, unsupervised.
    Once he was gone, she went directly
    Toward the leftmost of the rooms.
    'Neath where the Old Graf's portrait looms
    A chest stands. She recalled correctly
    The notes inside and seized the lot,
    Then brought it to this hiding spot.

13. It was a lengthy correspondence,
    She sees here, just between those two.
    She's jealous of the two respondents
    But starts, impatient to undo
    The ribbons tied around. She sifts the
    Worn papers, scans the writing, lifts the
    Signed copy of the pact away.
    What does the oldest letter say?
    "My Lord Graf: My name is Maria.
    I doubt that you remember me,
    But I was there that night to see
    You come before my father, he a
    Sworn enemy of yours, to bid
    Him make the deal with you he did."

14. Hold on. What deal? Is this referring
    To the accord? But Oma said
    Maria made that deal, occurring
    Upon her father's death, and led
    Them down a darkened path, and so on.
    This letter isn't much to go on,
    But here's the pact, and on the line,
    The Heller patriarch did sign.
    It seems her grandmother's portrayal
    Of these events is less than true.
    What happened? Did the deal fall through?
    Maria's note shows no betrayal
    So far, but Kinge reads with care
    The rest to find what truth is there.

15. "As you have honor, I beseech you
    Receive me ere this comes to woe.
    I've risked my father's wrath to reach you,
    And there is something you must know.
    To write it, though, would only worsen
    The problem. We must speak in person.
    You've read my words, and I shall wait
    For your response outside your gate."
    No answers here. To take such action
    Means something happened. Something bad.
    Now Kinge wishes that she had
    Some record of the Graf's reaction.
    But if he met her privately
    To talk, of course there wouldn't be.

16. Maria's suff'ring comes through clearly
     For all that. Kinge sees, at last,
     A feeling person there, not merely
     Some villainess from Oma's past.
     But while she feels tremendous pity
     For poor Maria, who was pretty
     Much her age when these lines were sent,
     Uncomfortably evident
     Is how the story parallels her
     Arrival here tonight. Suppose
     Romantic sentiments arose
     Back then as well? Her instinct tells her
     It cannot be, yet must concede
     There's plenty letters more to read.

17. "My Lord Graf: It is wrong to write to
     The architect of all my grief,
     But know I may explain my plight to
     No other and expect belief.
     When last I saw him, Papa glowered
     At me and said I was a coward,
     And he was right. How I have prayed
     For peace and found none. I've betrayed
     My father and I cannot bear it.
     My brothers are no help, and I
     Have no one else but you to try."
     The letter ends abruptly where it
     Met paper's edge and was dispatched
     Without, it seems, more leaves attached.

18. "Dear Graf: My mood has been so gloomy
    Of late, so dark my ev'ry thought.
    Your visit was a comfort to me,
    As was the golden cross you brought
    Me for a gift; the gesture humbles."
    Here Kinge ceases reading, fumbles
    Her pendant from its nesting place
    Beneath her collar. Face to face
    With only half the story, meaning
    Eludes her, and if there's a plan
    At work here, she's no closer than
    She was before to finding out. She's leaning
    Against the shelving, worn and sore,
    When comes a clicking from the door.

19. At this she holds herself so still she
    Can feel her thudding heartbeat slow
    Against her ribs. She waits until she
    Hears someone call her name below,
    Then breathes out. Doubtless he can hear her,
    And smell her, too. She edges nearer
    The wooden railing of her tier
    So he may see her. "I'm up here."
    The Graf looks up at her, not straying
    From where he stands, and nor does she
    Begin to leave the balcony.
    It's he first breaks the silence, saying,
    "Do tell me what you're doing, please."
    She shows the letters. "Reading these."

20. A page slips through her fingers, floating
    Down like a dying butterfly.
    He snatches it midair, and noting
    The writing, asks her, "Why so shy?
    These letters were not hidden from you."
    "I know," she answers, "But, how come you
    Gave her a necklace? What was she
    To you?" The Graf asks, teasingly,
    "Is that the cause of all this bother?
    I liked her well. And in the end,
    I think she might have called me friend."
    Says Kinge, "Though you killed her father?"
    As still as death the Graf's face falls.
    He turns and gestures to the walls.

21. "This all was open, mid-construction,
    In ninety-seven. I would say
    It was the site of introduction
    For Heller and his sons that day.
    Most hunters were a peasant nuisance,
    Or such had been my father's view since
    The Middle Ages. They were fair,
    Rewarding prey. He killed his share.
    Soon law and science had conspired
    With time to push such hunters out
    Of style. No longer so devout,
    They died, or fled, or else retired
    From digging in the village mud
    For kin they claimed drank human blood.

22. "Not Athanasius. Pragmatic
    Maria's father was, although
    By nature thoroughly fanatic,
    He did not fear my father, so
    Stout iron locks and reputation
    Were poor defense against invasion.
    Our human servants, hapless ones
    Fell first, cut down by Heller guns.
    From there, the pack of hunters headed
    Below to where my father slept
    Beside his Gräfin. Having crept
    Inside, they both of them beheaded.
    They left behind but scraps and ash,
    And pilfered treasures from our cache.

23. "I found the scene upon returning
    From buying books abroad. The air
    Hung thick with bitter smell of burning,
    The human dead still lying where
    They fell. My parents gone. My anger
    Would keep me from a mournful languor;
    With Timoch I began to track
    The author of this vile attack.
    It took some time to find the sinner,
    Which I used to devise a plan.
    His house we circled while the man
    Was home with all his kin for dinner.
    We sealed the back—a captive hunt—
    And let ourselves in through the front.

24. "His sons saw Timoch first and swarmed him
    Together, which was asinine.
    I seized Ath'nasius, disarmed him,
    And brought his wretched face to mine,
    Enjoying his distress. I wanted
    To crush his heart for how he'd flaunted
    His barb'rousness. And yet, would I
    Be gratified, to watch him die?
    Perhaps. What of his sons, his daughter?
    Alive, they might retaliate.
    But must I then obliterate
    Their line entire? Such pointless slaughter,
    For lifetimes, vengeance our excuse.
    I cast him down and whispered, 'Truce.'

25. "The man refused at first, as though he
    Had any choice. But I was firm.
    You've seen his signature. You know he
    Accepted, soon enough, my terms.
    Retreating to restore my castle,
    For months I had no word or hassle
    From them. I thought the problem solved.
    And here Maria got involved.
    Despite my mercy, Heller scorned me.
    His daughter came here to entreat
    Me, threw herself down at my feet
    And begged me for his life. She warned me
    In detail of his perfidy,
    His foolish plan to ambush me."

26. He pauses here, his head inclining,
    Then says: "Your ancestress was brave
    And honest, her worth far outshining
    The man whose life she sought to save.
    And I was touched by her emotion,
    Her tears, her filial devotion.
    I knew I never could forgive,
    But promised I would let him live.
    And from that night, she represented
    Her family. When she was gone?
    Her daughter, granddaughter, and on
    As long as her line lasts. Presented
    With Heller men's duplicity,
    I thought her sex might faithful be."

27. He smiles at Kinge, kindly. "Under
    The treaty, she and I were bound,
    But never lovers, Kunigunde."
    For moments, Kinge makes no sound.
    "What happened next?" she asks, unsteady.
    "He came for us. And we were ready.
    Alas for Athanasius,
    The sunlight was no let to us
    This time. We built a web of channels
    Throughout the castle. Using these,
    We tracked our enemy with ease.
    A false door here, some hidden panels…
    We trapped him in the very room
    His knife had made my parents' tomb."

28. She's listened to his tale unfold, her
    Eyes bright with tears. But something in
    His voice now makes her blood run colder;
    There's markèd paleness to his skin.
    "You've learned Luzia's vicious slander.
    She hates me, thus I understand her
    Desire to lie," he says. "But you?
    The woman I have taken to
    My heart?" His words throw shame upon her.
    "Not I, nor any of my kind
    Killed Athanasius. You'll mind,
    I am a creature ruled by honor
    And promises. Be satisfied
    With that, or not, as you decide."

29. The Graf completes his testimony.
    There's nothing Kinge thinks to say.
    He shakes his head, his visage stony,
    Then turns from her to walk away.
    "Don't go!" she calls, and now she's taking
    The stairs down, all her body shaking,
    To stand behind him, speaking low:
    "I'm sorry. Please. I didn't know.
    I am a Heller. You can't blame me
    For lies I've heard since I was two.
    But look at me! I'm here with you.
    I trust you. Georg." At his name, he
    Turns 'round to face her. He is proud,
    She knows, but looks him back, unbowed.

30. And then, the quiet still unbroken,
     He slowly folds her in his arms.
     Forgotten, any harsh words spoken;
     Forgiven, any thoughtless harms.
     "I wrote to you," he says, caressing
     Her hair. She quickly nods, professing,
     "I read your letter like a sign
     From heaven. I loved ev'ry line."
     He frowns at her. "But if you read it,
     Then why did you come here tonight?
     Maria's letters?" "No, not quite,"
     She says, "Your note was lovely, yet it
     Got one thing, one suggestion, wrong:
     I'm mortal. Waiting takes too long."

31. The Graf's strong arms like iron wreathing
     Her body, Kinge rests her head
     Against his chest, contented, breathing
     In deep his gorgeous fragrance, bred
     Of books and leather, oak and cedar,
     And candlewax. Beneath the sweeter
     Of these does Kunigunde mark
     A scent that's warm, alive, and dark.
     Somewhere inside, a tiny flicker
     Of longing she had never sensed
     So strong before now, pressed against
     His body, makes each breath come quicker.
     As if his thoughts with hers agree,
     They kiss each other eagerly.

32. "You're cold!" she sputters, so astonished
     She puts her palm across her lips.
     By his sad aspect then admonished,
     She says, "You're hungry," and she slips
     Her trembling hand in his, to warm it.
     She thinks a question, fights to form it
     Aloud. "Do you want me to go?"
     His fingers brush hers softly. "No."
     He must divine her thinking, yet he
     Wants her to say it, doesn't he?
     "Why don't you take some blood from me?"
     His smile for her is calm and steady.
     "A gracious offer, that, but why?"
     "I want you to. You're hungry, I…"

33. "You're curious. It is inviting,"
     He says, revealing teeth, "I fear
     My bite's perhaps not as exciting
     As you're imagining, my dear."
     A little part of Kinge panics.
     She's not considered the mechanics
     Of fangs and flesh in this whole flirt.
     She stammers, "How much does it hurt?"
     "A little. But I can…distract you."
     His gaze sweeps over her. Her face
     Grows hotter. Back to his embrace
     She goes. He asks, "Does that attract you?"
     "Oh, yes," she says. He nods. "I see.
     Then we'd best do this properly.

34. "But not here. Come!" She, trusting, harkens,
    And takes his lead as they depart,
    Through passages that twist and darken,
    To somewhere in the castle's heart
    Where lies a modest, cozy chamber.
    Its shadows black are poised to claim her
    'Til he lights candles in the dim,
    Which gild the room, the bed, and him.
    He strokes her face. Her human passion
    Makes heat enough for both; his touch
    Feels less cold. Any further such
    He stays, in gentlemanly fashion.
    "Before we can begin," says he,
    "Two questions you must answer me.

35. "The first is: Where? Where shall I bite you?"
    He rests his lips against her wrist.
    "Right here, perhaps. Would this delight you?"
    The soft skin tingles as it's kissed.
    "Inside your arm?" There, touches tickle.
    She bites her cheek as not to giggle.
    The Graf looks thoughtful. "Elsewhere, then."
    She quickly nods. "Yes. Try again."
    His kisses start anew, but slower.
    Beginning at her throat, they trace
    Her pendant's chain toward the place
    The diamond rests. A pause. Then lower.
    Her heart skips ov'r a beat or two.
    "Oh yes," she murmurs, "There will do."

36. Her dress slips from her shoulders, drifting
    To join his jacket, vest, and tie.
    He holds her to himself, and lifting
    Her to the bed, he comes to lie
    Beside her. She awaits him, and to
    Her great delight he moves his hand to
    Her hip and lightly rests it there.
    "The second question now, love: Where?"
    His hand she seizes in her yearning
    And guides to where she wants him best.
    His mouth he presses to her breast,
    The frisson from his kisses turning
    To lovely sweetness through her skin.
    She hardly feels his teeth go in.

37. There's pressure as the Graf continues
    To draw her blood, but no pain mars
    The singing in her very sinews;
    It builds, until the girl sees stars.
    Returned to Earth, but senses reeling,
    She reaches for her lover, feeling
    Warm skin beneath her fingertips,
    And tasting blood upon his lips.
    She's not sure what comes next. "So—should I…?"
    He stops her hand. "There is no need.
    I take my pleasure when I feed."
    "And, did you?" He but sighs, "How could I
    Describe you something so sublime?
    But get some rest. You're safe. There's time."

38.   Protesting, she already drowses;
     The pillow's downy pull is strong.
     Her sleep is dreamless. When she rouses,
     The candles show it wasn't long,
     But where is he? "Forgive me leaving."
     His voice seems near the door. "Believing
     You might be hungry once awake,
     I found some food, and this to slake
     Your thirst." She takes the proffered water
     And gratefully consumes a pear.
     He watches her, and she's aware
     Refreshment isn't all he's brought her:
     Maria's letters, newly bound
     With scarlet ribbon all around.

39.   "That's ev'ry letter. Should you heed them,"
     He says, "They'll tell you what is true.
     Take all the time you like to read them;
     I'm making them a gift to you."
     The gesture fills her heart to breaking.
     She can't forgive her Oma making
     Him out to be a monster, since
     She knows him, in his soul, a prince,
     And in his heart, a man. "You must be
     Off home," he whispers. "Let me stay
     With you," she begs. "I will some day,
     Some night," he says. "I want to, trust me.
     But problems here require my care,
     And Grandmother awaits elsewhere."

40. "She's horrible!" huffs Kinge as she
     Climbs out of bed and grabs her dress.
     "She has her reasons," he says. "Has she?
     I live with her, and it's my guess
     She just likes fighting and suspicion."
     He chuckles. "Family tradition."
     "But no, it doesn't have to be,"
     She says, and holds the letters he
     Has given her. "Maria knew that.
     My Oma's old and full of spite.
     When I'm in charge, I'll make it right."
     "I hope you get the chance to do that,"
     He says, his voice a mordant drawl.
     "Your Oma may outlive us all."

41. Her turn to laugh. He snuffs the candles
     As hand-in-hand they leave the room.
     She wonders at the way he handles
     The pathways through the night-dark gloom.
     But soon, though almost blind, she senses
     That something's wrong. The vampire tenses,
     Holds Kinge tighter, slows his strides.
     "Stay close," he tells her as he slides
     A panel open. Light comes glaring
     From gas lamps in the hall. The glint
     Is harsh enough to make her squint.
     The Graf is unaffected, staring
     At one approaching from ahead
     Who, seeing them appear, stops dead.

42. The Graf speaks first. "Good ev'ning, Galen."
     The man steps back, and bows. "My lord,"
     He mumbles in reply, so pale in
     The face, like he awaits the sword.
     "Explain yourself," the Graf says, dryly.
     But Galen looks at Kinge while he
     Attempts his master to appease.
     "I will, my lord, but not here. Please.
     Permit me to escort this lady
     Home first, and then…" "Oh, I think not."
     That voice roots Galen to the spot
     And Kinge, suddenly afraid he
     Might faint, says, "Yes. The choice is mine.
     Let Galen take me home. It's fine."

43. Her fingers press the vampire's arm. He
     Looks unconvinced. She says, "And I
     Am sure he wouldn't try to harm me.
     It's hard enough to say good-bye.
     Don't drag it out." She feels tears starting.
     His lips brush them away, imparting
     A tender kiss upon her cheek.
     She lifts her face to his to seek
     His mouth again, for one last fervent
     Farewell. He says, against her swoon:
     "Have courage. I will see you soon,"
     Then turns attention to his servant.
     "I think that I may bear your lack
     For one more hour. There and back."

44.   Like that, he's gone. She feels deserted,
      His words to her but little cheer;
      She turns to Galen. Eyes averted,
      He says, "Let's get you out of here."
      "Hold on!" He stops his walk. "What was it
      Between you two?" she asks. "Because it
      Sure sounded serious." A groan.
      "It's something I'll sort on my own,"
      He says. "The first of our concerns is
      That you're all right." She snaps, "I'm swell,"
      And hugs her chest. "So I can tell,"
      He says, his voice turned harsh. He turns his
      Regard away, heads down the hall,
      His coldness on her like a pall.

45.   He grips the leather of the steering
      Wheel tight. This ride, she hasn't said
      A single word within his hearing,
      But he feels eyes upon his head;
      It's screwing with his concentration.
      About to voice his irritation,
      He stops when she so quietly
      Asks, "Galen, are you mad at me?"
      He almost laughs, but she's in earnest.
      She says, "When I saw you today,
      You told me I should stay away
      From him." "And yet," he says, "my sternest
      Of warnings just meant squat to you.
      You're nineteen. Please. What else is new?"

46. He shrugs. "You made your own decision.
    It's pretty much what I'd have done
    At your age, and in your position.
    That's if there had been anyone
    To warn me then." Of course, there wasn't.
    He thinks she'll leave it there. She doesn't.
    She asks, "What's wrong?" At this, a seed
    Of something bursts in him, a need
    To speak aloud what he's been mulling
    Since last he bore his lady's bite,
    Since Kinge's smile in candlelight
    At St. Paul's church. He slows down, pulling
    The car upon the verge a ways.
    "I'm leaving Sternendach," he says.

47. "I'll drop you off and keep on driving
    The whole night through. I plan on one
    Quick stop for gas and food, arriving
    In Poland early, with the sun."
    No answer. Is this news so stunning?
    But then she says to him, "You're running
    Away!" and stares, her mouth agape.
    He says, "I'm making my escape.
    They'll hunt me, once they realize it.
    But with a nice head start, I could
    Get lost in some new place. I'm good
    At that, I hope. 'Cause otherwise it
    Won't matter. Still, I have to try."
    She shakes her head. "But Galen, why?"

48. "It's this," he starts his explanation.
    "You understand that this is my
    First honest human conversation
    In years? This here, with you. And I
    Want more." "From me?" she asks him, blinking.
    She presses 'gainst the car seat, shrinking
    As if afraid to get too close.
    "Not that," he chides her. "Don't be gross.
    I look at you, and I'm reminded
    Of all the many things I've lost
    To have this life. And it's a cost
    That, up to now, I never minded.
    But things have changed. I won't condemn
    Myself to live like this. Like *them*."

49. "I thought you loved her." There's such sadness
    In Kinge's eyes, it stings in his.
    He says, "You know, in all this madness,
    I do. But I know what she is."
    "If it's so bad," she says, demurely,
    "Then tell the Graf. He'd listen, surely."
    He laughs. "You heard the Graf, before.
    He doesn't trust me anymore.
    He'll kill me." "No," she says, "he couldn't.
    The pact." "Then he'll see me confined
    To dungeons 'til I lose my mind
    And kill myself." "You're wrong. He wouldn't,"
    She argues, "if he understood…"
    "Come on, now, Heller. Yes, he would."

50. This talk of dungeons slowly killing
     Turns icy fingers in his gut.
     He hides his face from her, unwilling
     To show his anguish. Open, shut,
     He hears her door behind him. Jolted
     By fears his young charge may have bolted,
     He curses. But she's back inside.
     She settles in the seat beside
     Him, looking at his face intently.
     "You're wrong about him, Galen. Take
     My word, this is a huge mistake.
     The Graf will help you." Confidently
     She lists his master's virtues, and
     Then reaches out to touch his hand.

51. Her words and touch both soothe and scald him.
     The girl sees with a lover's eyes,
     Like him, when Amy first enthralled him.
     Intoxicating, yes. But wise?
     Not very, no, and at this juncture
     He feels a pressing urge to puncture
     Her happy dreaming, quick and clean.
     "You are a child," he says. It's mean,
     And Kunigund' looks close to crying.
     She pulls away and sits there, dumb.
     He ponders what he has become,
     That he should find this satisfying.
     More reason he should disappear,
     He thinks, and throws the car in gear.

52. The Heller house soon darkly grows in
     The windows of the car. They're here.
     But Kunigunde sits there, frozen.
     "I'm sorry," Galen says, sincere.
     He almost hates to leave her, knowing
     What threats remain. "You're really going?"
     She asks, "Then who will I talk to?"
     Considering this point of view,
     He asks, "Why not come with me? Sunder
     All ties, be free?" "You're joking, right?"
     "Of course," he says. His throat feels tight.
     "Take care of yourself, Kunigunde."
     With that, there's nothing left to say.
     He lets her out and drives away.

53. Could anything she said prevent him
     From leaving? Now, to her chagrin,
     She'll never know. She does resent him
     For spoiling what 'til now had been
     A perfect night. 'S not like he likes her,
     Nor she him, but too late it strikes her
     That she and Galen are, if not
     Quite friends, the closest thing they've got.
     A deep breath in begins dispelling
     The weight that's gathered on her heart.
     The man is gone, and for her part,
     She'd rather spend her hours dwelling
     On all tonight that she has dared,
     On secrets learned, and pleasures shared.

54. "I'm home," breathes Kunigund' to no one,
    Relieved when no one answers back.
    The coast ahead is clear, although one
    Can't see but shadows in the black.
    She quickly sets about removing
    Her shoes, a silent tread improving
    The odds of getting up the stair
    Ere anybody knows she's there.
    She hears her doom before she sees it:
    The sharp click of a nearby switch.
    Luzia stands in lamplight, which
    Her glare makes cold enough to freeze it.
    And Kinge feels her innards twist,
    To see his letter in her fist.

Betrayals

The Graf's Letter:

The written word, like blood, maintains my life.
    Thus I, who have consumed so much of both
And in a world with sustenance so rife,
    Think meet I should the former aid in growth,
    And writing use to tender you an oath.

That such a course in honesty ensue,
    I wish a certain question to address.
You asked me once if I remembered you,
    The book of tales I gave you. I said yes.
    But this was less than truthful, I confess.

With ease, in fact, once you and I had met,
    I put you from my thoughts immediately.
Though just a child, you were Luzia's get.
    I'd see you soon enough, when you would be
    A weapon honed and trained to target me.

Suspicious, then, when I your note received,
    I feared a brand-new chapter in our war.
Were you Luzia's pawn, and I deceived?
    Or brave Maria, come to warn once more
    Of deadly Heller treachery in store?

A kindred spirit, one so young in years,
    Seemed too absurd a thought to entertain.
Instead I trapped you, challenged you, to tears,
    Subjecting you to coarse, unearned disdain.
    I shudder that I caused you so much pain.

You bared your heart to me that night, and proved
    Yourself the stronger, one who more would dare.
And how could I by this be aught but moved,
    I whom you captured in the Opera square
    With lovely, soulful eyes and plaited hair?

I've found with you in but a dozen nights
    Such joy as I had not to celebrate
For many years. Yet there remain delights
    We have not tasted and (though you may hate
    The word) for which we must in patience wait.

In time you will live on your own, and when
    You do, will we be far less vuln'rable.
It's safer that I not see you 'til then.
    Though not to think of you quite sensible
    Would be, it's also quite impossible.

I pray that you, who hold my heart and know
    My nature, in my promise here will trust.
Though none sees by which path our futures go,
    I'll wait as long as Fate decrees I must,
    And love you 'til the stars above are dust.

1. Luzia tries to read the missive,
   With steady voice, but it's a fight.
   "Perfection," she says, curt, dismissive.
   "I'll hand him this: the fiend can write."
   Her words of grudging admiration
   Belie the utter consternation
   Which all her soul like wildfire girds
   And leaves her struggling for words.
   First Galen at St. Paul's that morning
   To spy on them, which made no sense.
   That Kinge to the Graf's defense
   So suddenly arrived, was warning
   Enough that something was amiss.
   Yet she could not imagine this.

2. Or could she? Kunigunde clearly
   Is restless and too much alone,
   Which he, the Graf, has cavalierly
   Exploited. That's a heart of stone
   He has. Luzia should have brought her
   To Kisilova this year, taught her
   Out in the field, and kept her safe.
   But no. The girl would only chafe
   At that. She wants her independence,
   Some friends her age, a chance to court.
   She is a woman grown. In short,
   She wants the normal life descendants
   Of Heller line may not attain.
   Luzia knows too well the pain.

3. Does she embrace her grandchild, saying,
    "I love you, and I understand,"
    Forgiving her for disobeying,
    Forgoing wrath and reprimand?
    By no means. She has not forgotten
    Her fam'ly, nor her duty, not in
    A thousand years. She must redress
    The danger this girl's recklessness
    May now have brought upon them. Scowling,
    She puts compassion on the shelf.
    "Will you say nothing for yourself?"
    She asks, her words pitched low, like growling.
    But Kinge weathers this attack
    And says, "Give me my letter back."

4. The girl's eyes, stormy and accusing,
    Stir something in Luzia's mind,
    Who turns and stalks away, refusing
    To answer. Kinge's right behind
    Her as she hunts the kitchen, seeking
    A favorite cut-glass tumbler. Peeking
    Through cabinets reveals the flask
    Of kirsch. Thank God. Luzia asks,
    "Just tell me: what on Earth possessed you
    To write to him? His elegance?
    His beauty, his intelligence?
    Or was it pow'r and wealth impressed you?"
    Says Kunigund', indignantly,
    "I asked to see his library."

5.   Luzia scoffs at this and squeezes
     The glass rim tight, as if to test
     Its strength. Then from the flask she eases
     The cork. "Did he show you the rest?
     His dungeons, say?" Her hand is shaking.
     The bottle slips her fingers, breaking
     Her glass. She rashly disregards
     The danger in the spiky shards
     And pulls back, fingers cut and bloody.
     The wound—now splashed with brandy—stings,
     Reminding of unwelcome things.
     "You met the Graf first in his study,
     The gentleman he feigns to be.
     But I met him quite differently."

6.   She finds a cloth to stanch the bleeding.
     "I know this story," Kinge sighs,
     "This fairy tale that you've been feeding
     Me all these years. I know it's lies.
     The Graf, before I had to leave him,
     Explained what happened. I believe him.
     He didn't kill your Opa, nor
     Did any of his kind. He swore."
     Luzia says, "Of course, he'd sell you
     A tale that puts him in the right.
     It's even true, in certain light.
     But think, granddaughter. Did he tell you,
     In winning you to take his side,
     Exactly how the old man died?"

7.   The girl's face pales at this idea,
Her angry features brushed with doubt.
"You want this letter back?" Luzia
Displays it. "Then you hear me out."
The girl, reluctant, acquiesces.
Luzia on her bandage presses
And says, "There is, in his great hall,
A door. It's hidden in the wall,
And only vampires know to find it.
When I was seven, Timoch and
My mother, with me by the hand,
First led me through this door. Behind it
Are stairs that lead you only down,
In darkness and despair to drown.

8.   "He waited at the bottom level:
The Graf, below us, seemed to loom,
Emerging like a ghost or devil
And silent in that horrid gloom.
When his attention shifted to me
I felt his cold eyes boring through me
And shuddered. He just shook his head.
'I don't approve of this,' he said.
For once, my mother's will asserted
Itself. 'So you made clear to me.
She is his blood, Your Exc'llency,'
She said. 'I will not be diverted.'
We finished our descent to Hell,
To find her father in his cell."

9.   "His cell?" breathes Kunigund'. "He put him
      In prison?" There's a hint of fright
      Luzia savors. "Yes, and shut him
      Away from us, the world, and light.
      That dungeon cell was pestilential.
      The vampires covered his essential
      Requirements, let him have a bed.
      But he was cold and sparely fed."
      She won't say how he terrified her,
      His haunted, thin, unshaven face
      Before her in that awful place.
      She stuffs the mem'ry down inside her
      And finds herself a brand-new glass.
      A sip of kirsch; the feelings pass.

10.   She drinks again and says, "I'm grateful
      I got to know him, and that he
      Had time with me, despite the hateful
      Conditions. Ev'ry Sunday, we
      Would visit him. He told me stories
      About his long-lost hunting glories,
      Or tales of fam'ly, this and that,
      Ignoring Mother where she sat.
      Though Timoch did accompany us
      The first few years, to overhear
      Our talk, the Graf did not appear.
      He did see fit, in time, to free us
      From supervision. Absent strings,
      My Opa told me diff'rent things.

11. "He knew which weapons were efficient
And worth the effort to obtain.
He told me I'd become proficient
With them, if I could get to train
In Serbia with hunters. Telling
Me secrets, and the thought of felling
The Graf, spurred some recovery
Of strength in him. He trusted me.
I fantasized about how, one day,
When I was fully trained and grown,
I'd rescue him all on my own.
I went to him, that final Sunday,
To share my childish plans. Instead,
I found that he'd gone on ahead."

12. Luzia's kirsch glass rattles dully
Against the counter. Kinge stares.
It's obvious she doesn't fully
Believe the story. If she cares.
Luzia says, "There, in the ragged
And flick'ring light, I saw the jagged
Dark glass he'd used to make his end,
Still in his hand. I saw distend
A pool of blood, its odor seeming
So thick you'd taste it in the air.
That smell soon brought the vampires there.
While Timoch calmed my mother's screaming,
The Graf his monst'rous nature proved
And watched, unmoving and unmoved."

13. She grits her teeth, her heartbeat quickened
     By shame and fear that still won't fade.
     The Graf did this to them. She's sickened
     That he has yet to be repaid.
     The girl toys with her pendant idly
     A moment. Then she answers, snidely,
     "If truly that's what you observed,
     Sounds like he got what he deserved."
     Luzia fights the urge to hit her,
     And tear that diamond from its chain.
     Instead, she says with deep disdain,
     "I see he's given you some glitter.
     My mother also let him buy
     Her off with gold, and she'd comply."

14. "What's wrong with you?" asks Kinge, letting
     The pendant fall, as if it burns.
     She finds unvarnished truth upsetting?
     Well, good. It's long past time she learns.
     Luzia says, "I was eleven
     When all this happened. It was seven
     Years more 'til I joined Stepan's crew.
     He taught me hunting, working through
     The finest weapons then invented,
     The classics. I learned ev'ry one:
     The sword, the axe, my Opa's gun.
     But I was never quite contented.
     To kill the Graf, I knew, would take
     Far more than training and a stake.

15. "No blade or gun goes undetected
    By Timoch past the castle doors.
    So I need something unexpected.
    With Stepan, I've concocted scores
    Of plans, designs, and I've discarded
    Them all. The Graf is too well-guarded."
    She waves the letter, says "It's clear
    The answer's what he's written here.
    Because the Graf is right about you:
    You are a weapon, whose design
    Is his invention, dear, not mine.
    I cannot take him down without you.
    Help me, and you can free us all."
    Luzia lets the letter fall,

16. But Kinge neatly bends to stop it.
    From somewhere she pulls out a wad
    Of papers, puts this one atop it,
    And stands back up. "I swear to God,"
    She says, "I will not help you hurt him.
    Not ever. Why would I desert him
    When he loves me?" "My girl, wake up!"
    Luzia barks, and slams her cup.
    It stays intact, but Kinge flinches.
    "Does anything I've told you of
    That creature show that he can love?
    He's happy killing us by inches.
    My mother, son, whatever spell
    Had caught them, now has you as well."

17. She stops then, hearing something muffled
     Behind her, and she turns around.
     The sound was Eva, who has shuffled
     Downstairs, clad in her dressing gown.
     "What's going on?" asks Eva, gravely,
     Arms crossed before Luzia bravely.
     So focused and awake, she shows
     A fire despite her sleep-pressed clothes
     And hair. Luzia, irritated,
     Tries shooing her toward the door.
     "It's fam'ly business. Nothing more."
     Says Eva, unintimidated:
     "I'm fam'ly too. You made me so
     When you gave me my pistol, no?"

18. Then Eva moves to Kinge, brushes
     A stray hair from her daughter's brow.
     Her finger to her lips, she shushes
     Luzia's protest. "I'll speak now.
     My daughter isn't yours to order
     Around. She's my child. I support her."
     The other snaps, "I'm sure you're right.
     She tell you where she was tonight?"
     While Kinge gasps, Luzia snatches
     With blinding speed the billet-doux
     And hands it off to Eva, who
     Starts reading while her daughter watches.
     A silence thick as tar descends
     While Eva with the note contends.

19. First Eva takes a breath and holds it,
     Then, hissing through her teeth, exhales.
     She sets the letter down, re-folds it,
     And scores the creases with her nails.
     Another breath. Her finger grazes
     The paper one more time. She raises
     Her dark eyes. Something in them, raw,
     Shoots venom at her moth'r-in-law.
     "Please tell me why you came back early,"
     She says. "To make us mis'rable?
     If so, your plan was masterful.
     Or were you just so terse and surly
     That Stepan and his retinue
     Had finally had enough of you?"

20. She's fishing with that accusation,
     Luzia knows, but still is bruised.
     And Eva's face, in her vexation,
     Is like the one Maria used
     Against her daughter, when they feuded.
     But Eva isn't finished. "You did
     The same thing when my husband pried
     Himself away from you. He tried
     To reason, but you wouldn't listen.
     My God! How you would carry on,
     The two of you. And now he's gone.
     You somehow blame the Graf for this, in
     That way that everything's his fault.
     But really, you're as coarse as salt."

21. The battle's joined. The girl's eyes widen.
     The older women stare and seethe,
     No old politeness left to hide in.
     And Kunigund', the first to breathe,
     Says, "I found Papa's medal. Oma
     Has hid it in her office. Mama,
     I meant to tell, eventually…"
     "Oh, Kinge, please. Don't talk to me."
     Then Eva shuts her eyes and, sliding
     The letter 'cross the counter to
     Her daughter's hand, she speaks anew.
     "The Graf is not the one dividing
     Our family, Luzia. Thus
     You'll get no fighting help from us."

22. Luzia snorts. The hell with Eva.
     Why waste her time with one so weak?
     This fight has made her come to crave a
     More sating outlet for her pique.
     "It's mutiny?" She smiles. It's mirthless.
     She says to Kinge, "Words are worthless.
     Decisions—actions—open doors.
     You want him all that much? He's yours."
     She pulls her weapon from its holster:
     Her Opa's gun, which he bestowed
     On her. She pauses to unload
     This relic she has used to bolster
     Her courage and authority,
     Then lays it down decisively.

23. "I hereby forfeit my position
    As liaison to you, my heir.
    You lead us, if you have ambition,
    And we will see if you can bear
    That weighty burden any better
    Than I." Says Eva, "I won't let her."
    "It's not your choice. It never was,"
    Luzia says. "See what she does
    When her beloved Graf betrays her—
    For his inhumanness will tell—
    And she must carry that as well."
    The girl says nothing. Did this faze her?
    Luzia smiles to think she's won.
    Then Kunigund' picks up the gun.

24. It's old and heavy, but she'll manage.
    She checks the chamber, cylinder.
    This weapon will do no more damage
    Now its command belongs to her.
    She tells her Oma, "Yes, I'll do it.
    I'll lead our side, instead of you. It
    Looks like you've done it much too long."
    "And do you really think you're strong
    Enough for that?" Luzia fences,
    And Kinge finds it bittersweet
    To watch her wrestle with defeat
    But, like her Oma, she dispenses
    No pity; she can't give a damn.
    "You've no idea how strong I am."

25. Her grandmother and mother tussle
    Some more. They hiss, they snap, they shout.
    It fades to but a distant rustle
    As Kunigunde tunes them out.
    The letters from the Graf she seizes
    And holds them to her heart. It pleases
    Her not to think of Oma's mess,
    But revel in the night's success—
    One hour, all her prospects brightened,
    Like Fate has given her a gift.
    Her thoughts despite this fortune shift
    To Galen, last seen lost and frightened.
    What kind of solace will he find
    When he leaves Sternendach behind?

26. He meant to drive to Poland. Honest.
    With Kunigunde safely dropped
    At home he started off, and promised
    Himself he would, before he stopped,
    At least have gotten to the border.
    He has his papers all in order
    And, from a secret, private stash
    He's gathered quite a chunk of cash.
    There's nothing else he needs to save him.
    The weather's clear, the car is gassed
    And ready, and he's long since passed
    The hour's grace his master gave him.
    The open road should lie ahead.
    So why's the castle there instead?

27. A subject to the force of habit,
    He drove here in a blurry trance.
    He freezes like a startled rabbit.
    He's lived here twenty years. Perchance
    The castle has him on a tether,
    Invisible, but tough as leather,
    Which will not let him go astray.
    He should have run by light of day!
    To try at night compounds the error
    Of thinking anyone could hide
    From Timoch, who may stalk outside,
    In shadows dark. The simple terror
    That he will be discovered grips
    His heart, which sev'ral pulses skips.

28. But nothing happens. Galen gnashes
    His teeth, and then his nerves dissolve
    In fresh adrenaline, which splashes
    A fatal chill on his resolve.
    He presses the accelerator,
    And checks the… Christ, it's even later
    Than he imagined. How'd he waste
    So many hours in his haste
    Tonight to bite the hand that feeds him?
    The brakes again. So will he just
    Desert the Graf, whose cautious trust
    He worked so long to earn? He needs him.
    The man knows, too, he won't get far
    In this, his master's stolen car.

29. In much this manner Galen dithers,
    Until the east glows pink and blue
    And all the heavens' starlight withers.
    He parks the car and heads in through
    The castle doors. The halls are quiet
    With morning calm. He can't deny it:
    He loves this time of day, this peace.
    It feels like home. Such musings cease
    When he detects the blend of honey
    And cloves come wafting from his rooms.
    No matter how he swears and fumes
    He knows, deep down, no threat nor money
    Could stop him following that scent.
    This, too, is home. Perhaps it's meant.

30. He does not greet her when he enters,
    Though lamps he switches on reveal
    Her in his chair. Instead he centers
    His focus on the curtains' seal.
    He chokes off strands of daylight straying
    Through any cracks, then turns round, saying,
    "It's day. You should be in your bed!"
    She smiles at him. "So Timoch said.
    But I don't take his orders, darling.
    Nor yours." At once her smile goes flat,
    And when the man recoils from that
    Her pretty features turn to snarling.
    "Your presence here was missed tonight.
    I almost thought you'd taken flight."

31. "I'm here, aren't I?" It's not convincing,
    This truth that quavers like a lie.
    Indeed, the Gräfin frowns, evincing
    No confidence in his reply.
    She says, "The girl was here." "I know that.
    He had me drive her home. Although that
    Was my idea." "Yes, no doubt,"
    She purrs. "What did you talk about
    While on this drive?" He shifts, uneasy.
    "We talked of life, my lady. Dreams.
    How love costs more than first it seems."
    The Gräfin's stare makes Galen queasy.
    "So now you're a philosopher,"
    She says. "Are you in love with her?"

32. And there it is, her eyes perceiving
    What he had not the nerve to say:
    The reason he's resisted leaving.
    The reason why he cannot stay.
    "I'm not," he says, and isn't lying.
    "You're perfect, beautiful, undying,
    And I have only ever been
    In love with you. But I feel kin
    To Kunigund', and my affection
    For her comes from a diff'rent place.
    I know the heartaches she may face,
    And all the wonders. That connection…
    To tell the truth, it thrills me, and
    It's nothing you can understand.

33. "The girl is young. I've no illusion
     She cares for me, and that's as well.
     But staying here, in this seclusion
     From my own kind, will not dispel
     My need for one to know and love me.
     My lady, you're so far above me
     You cannot give me that, and so
     I beg you, Amy. Let me go."
     A tear slips down her cheek. Amazing.
     He didn't think her kind could cry.
     He pulls her in his arms, to try
     To comfort her, her fang teeth grazing
     His throat. Amata holds him tight.
     He'll give her this: just one more bite.

34. Familiar pain, those needles pricking
     His flesh, but then she twists her head
     And pushes Galen from her, licking
     From off her lips a splash of red.
     He looks at her, in shock, refusing
     At first to note the warmth diffusing
     Down 'cross his chest. A chilling damp
     Comes next. He brings his hand to clamp
     Against the wound. Lightheaded, falling,
     He cries out as he hits the floor,
     Which only causes blood to pour
     More quickly. With no strength for crawling,
     He prays for help, receiving none.
     A cold voice gasps, "What have you done?"

35. The Graf observes, transfixed with horror,
    The Gräfin's bloodied mouth, and worse,
    The human's fallen form before her.
    He distantly hears Timoch curse
    Before his vassal kneels, inspecting
    The victim. But the Graf, expecting
    No hope, dares not wish otherwise.
    And now he comes to recognize
    How badly he miscalculated.
    He knew the Gräfin's jealousy,
    Directed all his energy
    To shielding Kunigund'. He rated
    No threat to Galen from his wife,
    And this has cost the man his life.

36. One cannot fathom why she killed him.
    She asked to turn him, did she not?
    Or has she permanently stilled him
    To hide his role in some dark plot?
    Where's Kunigund'? The Graf's heart lurches.
    Did she reach home? By day, a search is
    Impossible; no way to know.
    She's safe. He must believe her so.
    What will she think of what's transpired?
    And more, what will Luzia do
    To him, the Graf, who's now seen two
    Poor humans in his care expired?
    The Gräfin, Devil take her gall,
    May well tonight have ruined all.

37. "What have you done?" he bellows, baring
    His teeth. He takes her by the wrists
    And sharply tugs her close, not caring
    A jot how feebly she resists.
    Against the chest of drawers he slams her,
    While with his eyes and words he damns her.
    Then, cutting through the air like blades,
    Comes Timoch's whisper, "Sire, he fades."
    Alive? Yes. Timoch's stopped the bleeding.
    The Graf can hear the dismal thud
    Of Galen's heart. Too little blood.
    The signs of life are fast receding
    And when they're gone? Catastrophe.
    What other option can there be?

38. "Hold her," he says to Timoch, taking
    His place by Galen on the ground.
    He checks his pulse and lifts him, making
    One last attempt to bring him 'round.
    But Galen's breath, in tatters coming,
    Soon stops completely. He's succumbing.
    Like lead the man's head sinks to rest
    Against the vampire's arm and chest.
    The Graf feels wrath and sorrow rending
    His heart; he last held her like this,
    His Kunigund', in love and bliss.
    "Forgive me, please," he whispers. Sending
    His fangs into his palm, he drips
    Dark lifeblood over Galen's lips.

39. The man's mouth twitches faintly, catches
    The ichor. At a thimbleful
    His eyes snap open. Galen latches
    Upon the wound and starts to pull
    More blood. And more. And each pull stronger.
    The Graf can't let him drink much longer.
    Already cold creeps from the bite
    Along his arm. He fears what might
    The outcome be if that chill reaches
    His heart. But Galen soon falls free
    And starts to writhe. It's agony
    The Graf remembers, change that leaches
    Humanity from flesh and bone.
    What might remain, remains unknown.

40. That's if it works, the new blood flooding
    His veins. The Graf leans in to look
    In Galen's mouth, where fangs are budding.
    The Graf sighs in relief. It took.
    To Galen's rising cries he deafens
    Himself, and also to the Gräfin's
    More muted protest. Rising straight,
    He fears his legs won't bear his weight,
    And Timoch quickly steps to lend him
    His arm. The two exchange a glance.
    The Graf resumes his lordly stance
    And says: "Release her. Let her tend him."
    His hand gives tiny, throbbing pains.
    The wound has healed. The cold remains.

41. Now Galen's screams have dimmed to choking
     And heaving sobs. Beside him, stained
     With tears and blood, the Gräfin's stroking
     His hair, her visage pale and pained.
     This image fills the Graf with loathing,
     As does his clammy, gore-soaked clothing
     And white skin. He must look the beast.
     But Galen's life is saved, at least.
     No more can he read Timoch's thinking
     Than see the sun through stone; no less
     He feels them both, as if they press
     Upon his skull. He takes unblinking
     Assessment of the day's events.
     It's time to ready their defense.

42. "It happened this way. She presented
     To me her wish to turn this man."
     He falters briefly. "I consented.
     At dawn this morning she began
     To drain his life from him, unaided.
     I was her witness when she traded
     Her blood for his. I have endowed
     Him with a fief, and he has vowed
     To me in turn his faithful service."
     At this announcement, Timoch nods
     Serene acceptance, quite at odds
     With how the Gräfin looks more nervous
     With ev'ry word she hears him speak.
     He ponders punishments to wreak.

43. He spits at her, "Congratulations.
    You've gotten what you asked of me,
    My lady. And as your creation,
    He's your responsibility.
    Teach Galen what he needs to know to
    Survive in Sternendach and so, too,
    Will you improve your flagging skill
    At taking blood without the kill.
    Once he's learned to my satisfaction,
    Then you, Amata…you are out.
    Leave Sternendach by any route
    You like." Such payment for her action
    Sounds easy, but he sees she gleans
    His point. She knows what exile means.

44. "You'd cut me off from your protection?"
    She says. "The hunters will pursue
    Me then! You promised me…" "Correction:
    I bargained, Madam, as did you.
    You broke the rule you swore to follow.
    Our bargain thus is void." She swallows.
    "I'll tell the Hellers that you lie,"
    She says. "Do that. I'll tell them why,"
    He answers, "Please, if you prefer it,
    We'll tell Luzia ev'rything
    And she, the Heller Wolf, can bring
    Your doom tonight. Shall we defer it?"
    She cradles Galen on her knees,
    And nods to show that she agrees.

45. The lateness and the blood loss weighing,
    The Graf's limbs feel like so much sand.
    He must leave ere the room starts swaying,
    And while he has the strength to stand.
    "Sleep here with him today, Amata,"
    He orders, "When night falls, allot a
    Short leash to him, for all our sakes.
    He will be hungry when he wakes.
    And then the mess in here wants cleaning."
    With one last look, he steps outside
    And stumbles. Timoch, close beside
    Him, stays his fall. The Graf knows, leaning
    On him, he need no more pretend.
    "What have I done?" he asks his friend.

46. Says Timoch then, "You must preserve this
    Frail peace for which you've so long fought."
    "But Galen. He did not deserve this."
    "No, Sire," says Timoch, "He did not."
    "And I must write Luzia, later,"
    The Graf says, "Pray my lie will sate her."
    He hangs his head. "Must I begin
    Deception now?" "It's no great sin
    To lie," says Timoch, "if your cause is
    Your own defense. And such as she
    Has not earned perfect honesty."
    "It's not just her." Here Timoch pauses,
    And says, "It's not a thing you planned.
    But Kunigund' would understand."

47. The Graf says nothing to this facile
Response, but lets himself be led
Through hidden pathways of the castle.
"I love her, Timoch." "As you've said.
But if the truth should give Luzia
A pretext for revenge, I see a
Disaster on our heads may break.
What difference would your feelings make?"
"Enough," the Graf says, as they enter
Within the secret bedroom, where
He brought the girl and, he would swear
These hours later, still can scent her.
He sorrows as he gains his bed
And sleeps like any restless dead.

Choices

1. At this time, near the change of season,
    The stars come earlier to fill
    The sky and brighter burn, good reason
    To watch them shine and spite the chill.
    Just so tonight. The castle tower
    Stands empty at the ev'ning hour,
    However. Down the spiral stairs,
    Within the library, there flares
    A tended fire. The Graf is warming
    His hands before the vivid flame.
    For reasons which he will not name
    Aloud, he sits alone, performing
    Some ritual of heat and light
    In preparation for this night.

2.   He wrote Luzia, as intended,
      Right after Galen's brush with death,
      A detail here and there amended
      Of why he drew his final breath.
      Congruent with his expectation,
      A Heller note of confirmation
      Arrived soon after. He would find
      It was by Kunigunde signed.
      He wonders if he should have gauged it
      A warning. Then, he nearly wept
      To see her name. Such fear had crept
      Within his thoughts, and this assuaged it.
      His love safe, none could judge him for
      The fault of seeing nothing more.

3.   "I have to see you. I'm proposing
      We meet at seven, three nights hence.
      The usual place," she wrote in closing.
      And that's tonight. His mood is tense.
      Perhaps it's Galen's circumstances.
      Amata's efforts to advance his
      Adjustment were consid'rable;
      He almost is presentable.
      No, Galen's not the problem, is he?
      While he might easily be shunned,
      The Graf must meet with Kunigund'
      Alone, and this has kept him busy
      Consuming extra pints of blood
      And setting match to firewood.

4. He rubs his palm—the flesh there twinges.
    He's taken from his reverie
    By knocking, and the creak of hinges.
    Her voice says, softly, "Exc'llency?"
    And there she stands, his angel, seeming
    More beautiful than all his dreaming
    Of her these days apart. Her eyes,
    Though, wound. He wills himself to rise
    And offer her his hand, reminding
    Himself: there is no cold, no mark,
    No vestige of that deed so dark.
    He gasps as they make contact, finding
    Just how misplaced his worry is.
    Her hand is frostier than his.

5. Relieved that she does not refuse him
    Her touch, he nonetheless detects
    Some alterations which confuse him
    In her appearance and effects.
    She's wearing clothing which, he posits,
    Came from the back of Eva's closets:
    A wool suit, drab and flavorless.
    He rather misses that green dress.
    The jacket's open…where's her pendant?
    The diamond's gone. Now hanging there,
    A cross that he'd know anywhere—
    Maria's. Borne by her descendant,
    It triggers in him some malaise.
    "Tell me what's happened, love," he says.

6. "I take it you received my letter,"
    Says Kunigund'. "The bottom line
    Is Oma has stepped down as head. Her
    Responsibilities are mine."
    He's shocked. "Luzia abdicated?
    Whatever could have motivated…?"
    "She found the letter that you sent
    To me. This is her punishment."
    The girl's deep frown and redness rimming
    Her eyelids tell him she agrees,
    Though God knows why. The vampire sees
    This change a hopeful future limning
    For both of them, an open way.
    He asks, "What does your mother say?"

7. She reddens, turns. Did he embarrass
    Her with his words? What more is wrong?
    She says, "My mother is in Paris.
    And no, I don't know for how long.
    Could be forever." Here she shudders,
    And hugs herself. The vampire utters
    No words, but simply marks her pain
    And gives the girl room to explain.
    "My mother said that this existence,
    This secret war, was just a trap.
    I'm glad to know it didn't snap
    On her, and she can get the distance
    She wants so much." She stands in place.
    He wishes he could see her face.

8.   She says, "But that's not why I came here."
He bluntly, lest he misconstrue
Her meaning, asks, "What is your aim here?"
She whirls to face him. "How could you
Do that to him, against his wishes?
To Galen? Are you that malicious?"
Her rage, the fire. The room grows hot.
"Please sit," he tells her. "I will not!"
She paces back and forth, eschewing
The comfort offered her. "You stole
His life," she says. "For what? Control?"
He bristles. "'Twas the Gräfin's doing,"
He says. "Despite what you imply,
It's she deserves your ire. Not I."

9.   "But she required your permission,"
She answers, "and your letter said
You gave it, of your own volition.
You are the Graf. It's on your head."
This stings him, yet it serves to show him
How deeply she has come to know him;
Her words, in righteous anger spilt,
Reflect his own view of his guilt.
But cautious, prideful, he won't show this.
She asks him, "Did you…see this done
Because you knew he planned to run
Away that night?" He did not know this.
If she did…oh, tormenting doubt.
He could have let the man bleed out.

10. "If he ran, I would not prevent him,"
    The Graf says. "This, at least, is true.
    But Galen didn't run. What sent him
    Back home to us when he was through
    Escorting you?" And something alters
    In Kinge's eyes. Her anger falters;
    Her tough expression starts to crack.
    She tells him, "I made him go back,"
    With shaking breath. "When Galen said you
    Would murder him, his fear was real,
    But I told him he should appeal
    To you. You'd help him. And instead, you
    Have damned him, and made me a fool.
    Just tell me why you'd be so cruel."

11. "Oh, Kunigund'." He would caress her,
    Tell everything, put all to rights
    With her, his lover and confessor.
    But then he catches, hard and bright,
    Her cross's gleam, and it repels him.
    No matter how his heart compels him,
    He may, if this is how things are,
    A Heller only trust so far,
    With so much truth. He tells her, "There're
    Things you don't know. I made the call
    That caused the least death. That is all
    I've done for seven decades. Error
    In this means, simply, our peace fails.
    That is what being Graf entails."

12. She's quiet. Is this declaration
    Of his enough to mollify?
    "So, Galen was a calculation?"
    She asks, lip trembling. "What was I?"
    "You ask me that?" Of course, she has to.
    He would not be so foolish as to
    Expect her faith in them abides
    Suspicion from so many sides.
    "You are," he says, "a valiant beauty.
    That has not changed, and never will.
    No calculus does that fulfill.
    Your love distracted me from duty,
    From cynic thoughts and lonesome moods.
    You were…redemption," he concludes.

13. As if she finds this all too wearing,
    She sinks into a plush bergère,
    Her focus distant. Firelight flaring
    Brings burnished highlights to her hair.
    She gazes at the fireplace, stilly,
    And says, "It feels a little silly
    To ask about eternity.
    But had you thought of turning me?"
    She picks at loose threads in the battered
    Upholst'ry. It may be he had,
    He might. "Would you have wanted that?"
    He asks. She says, "Would that have mattered?"
    He hisses softly as this dart
    Strikes true, its poison in his heart.

14. Her look of triumph soon collapses,
    Her eyes screwed tightly shut. A pang
    Of guilt or grief the cause perhaps is—
    Soon tears upon her lashes hang.
    "I'm sorry. God, I've done this badly,"
    She says, breathes deeply. "I would gladly
    Go back to how we were before.
    I think this week that I've learned more
    About my fam'ly than I care to.
    But neither are your hands so clean.
    This role I took puts me between
    You both. I don't have anywhere to
    Escape to. Like my mother said,
    I'm trapped." She sniffs and hangs her head.

15. The Graf says, softly, "You were weeping
    Your first night here with me. To dry
    Those eyes, I do remember sweeping
    Us up the stairs to see the sky,
    And 'neath that canopy I kissed you."
    He sighs. "For I could not resist you.
    You said that night that we were free."
    "And you were right to laugh at me."
    Her speech, so sad and weary, causes
    His very soul to ache. He feels
    Such tenderness for her, he kneels.
    "I wasn't, Kunigund'." He pauses,
    And with his fingers, lifts her chin.
    "We're freer than we've ever been."

16.   She pulls her head back. "I've been reading,"
      She says, "About his suicide."
      "Ath'nasius?" he says, conceding.
      "The details would have been inside…"
      "…Maria's letters. Yes. Took ages
      To read them through. In all those pages
      She never once assigned you blame
      For his demise. But all the same,
      There's something diff'rent, almost brittle
      In what she wrote you once he died.
      If she called you her friend, she lied;
      Maria feared you, just a little."
      The Graf looks down. This last he long
      Had thought, but hoped that he was wrong.

17.   He says, "The manner of his dying
      I, to this night, do much regret,
      And, too, its part in multiplying
      Maria's grief. She was beset
      By troubles that her father brought her.
      I know it also scarred her daughter,
      And I am sorry." "Yes, she knew,"
      Says Kunigund', "and I do, too.
      It's just…" Then, looking apprehensive,
      She trails off. "After all we've done,"
      He asks, surprised, "belovèd one,
      Do you fear me?" Her face turns pensive,
      A shadow falling like a hood.
      "No more," she tells him, "than I should."

18. "I see." The Graf, in his dejection,
    Sits back and rests upon his heels.
    He contemplates the next direction
    For him and her—there's one. He steels
    Himself against the blow that's coming.
    He hears their hearts in frantic drumming,
    Together now, but ne'er again,
    And says, "You do not love me, then."
    While it would shame him to admit it,
    He cannot bear to look at her
    While she responds. He hears her stir
    Against the velvet. Then she's quitted
    Her armchair, slowly sinking down
    To join him, kneeling on the ground.

19. He breathes her fragrance, feels her twining
    Her fingers through his hair. Her touch
    Is soft, but it insists. Divining
    Her want, he reaches out to clutch
    Her shoulders. Kunigunde kisses
    Him so intensely that, if this is
    The last time, he would soon delay
    Its end. As tightly as he may,
    He holds her, feeling such completeness.
    Some moments pass. The kisses stop,
    And from her eye a single drop
    Lands on his lips. It bears the sweetness
    He'd tasted in the blood she gave
    Him, sweetness he has come to crave.

20. "Don't go," he whispers, feeling newly
     Courageous, "Please, we've come so far."
     She says, "I love you, Georg, truly
     I do. But I know what you are."
     She kisses him once more, her lashes
     Against his cheek. They feel like ashes,
     The kiss like…nothing. She withdraws
     And gains her feet. Without a pause
     She turns to leave him. He would never
     Insist she stay. She knows her mind,
     And that he loves, though left behind
     Is some soft part of her forever.
     All good on balance but, bereft,
     He wonders if there's one thing left.

21. "Frau Heller!" calls the vampire to her.
     She turns and waits before the doors.
     He rises, but does not pursue her.
     He says, "My library is yours
     To visit as the spirit moves you.
     And should you think that it behooves you
     To talk, some night, of poetry
     Or music, then would I agree."
     A breathless moment while she muses.
     She smiles, a little. "Possibly,
     In time. My thanks, Your Exc'llency."
     He nods. It will be as she chooses.
     He bows before her, whereupon
     The doors sweep open, and she's gone.

22. She makes it twenty paces. Gripping
    A molded archway for support,
    She feels her sweaty fingers slipping
    Against the wood. Her breaths come short
    And fast, and she can't comprehend it.
    Did she not come back here to end it?
    To look the vampire in the eye
    And tell him they were through? Then why,
    With all she knows, why does this ardor
    Persist, which she should disavow?
    Why does she miss him, even now?
    And why did she think he'd fight harder
    To keep her? This was her success,
    And leaves her heartsick nonetheless.

23. This stupid jacket's fabric itches.
    Oh, how on Earth will she survive
    The path she's chosen, if the hitch is
    That she must frequently contrive
    To meet with him, but not as lovers
    (And well before her heart recovers)
    To talk of treaties, wars, and hunts?
    She wishes that she had, just once,
    Her Oma's practiced knack for closing
    Emotions down at times like these,
    If not her painful memories.
    She smooths her skirt and sighs, supposing
    She's caught the worst this night can throw.
    "Nice outfit, kid. Does Mother know?"

24. She finds the stomach not to shatter
    As he, in his familiar style,
    Approaches her and starts to natter.
    "Well, Kunigund'. It's been a while,"
    Says Galen. "I was not expecting
    To see you—not that I'm objecting.
    Thought you'd be in the library
    With… Come on, you can look at me."
    He speaks so casually, she forces
    Herself to turn and take him in.
    He still wears that annoying grin.
    The line of teeth it shows, of course, is
    Much changed, and it's an awful sight,
    His brand-new fangs so sharp and white.

25. His flesh, however, that's turned duller,
    His handsome face turned gaunt, all planes
    And shadows washed of human color,
    Picked out in spots with darker veins.
    She realizes she's been dreading
    This meeting with him. Galen, spreading
    His arms out, asks, "Well, what d'you think?"
    The question brings her to the brink
    Of tears again. She almost buckles.
    Somehow she manages to say,
    "Oh, God. Oh, Galen, why did they
    Do this to you?" But Galen chuckles
    As he replies, his glance askew,
    "They did it 'cause I asked them to."

26. It's possible that he keeps talking.
    She can't be sure; a droning whine
    Sounds in her ears. She stands there, gawking,
    A tightness pulling at her spine,
    And strains for sense. There isn't any.
    He told her things, perhaps too many
    Those nights ago, when last he warned
    Her from this place, and bleakly mourned
    The life he lived among these creatures.
    She blinks and tries to wrap her head
    Around this. "That's not right. You said…"
    He looks at her with blankened features,
    Then smiles what might be sympathy.
    "Of course. You're jealous they chose me."

27. "I'm what?" she sputters. "That's deluded!
    I never wanted…" "Is that so?"
    Perhaps. The thought, now quite precluded,
    Had never had the chance to grow.
    He says to her, "My claim was stronger
    Than yours because I've been here longer.
    My lady's love is not a game
    She plays. Now, can you say the same
    For him? And if another gap in
    The roster comes along? You're young.
    Can you be sure you'll still be hung
    On him by then? Strange things do happen.
    I like you human, anyway.
    It suits me if that's how you stay."

28. This thing, so close she almost smells him,
     Is not her friend. It makes her sick.
     "Just stay away from me," she tells him.
     His teeth close with an icy click.
     "What's wrong?" he asks her, softly. "Might you
     Be scared that I would try to bite you,
     As if I can't control my thirst?
     I'm sure I wouldn't be the first."
     Then, suddenly, like thunder cracking,
     A door slams in the hall, from where
     The Gräfin scowls upon the pair
     Of them. Her look sends Galen backing
     Away from Kunigund', who draws
     A thin breath through her tight-clenched jaws.

29. The Gräfin, like a prison warder,
     Her footsteps pounding on the floor,
     To Galen barks, "You heard the order.
     The Hellers, none of them, are your
     Concern. Don't talk to her. I hear she
     Is Heller chief now, and I fear she
     Has not your interests at heart,
     If once she did." His pale lips part,
     Then close. He looks disoriented.
     The Gräfin's fingers brush his cheek
     As she leans in to him, to speak
     Words in his ear. By these contented,
     It seems, he bends to kiss her hands
     And leaves without a backward glance.

30. She almost follows him. She nearly
     Calls out to her lost friend, but shame
     Has paralyzed her so severely
     She cannot even say his name.
     This is her fault. When he confided
     His plan to leave, well, she decided
     That she knew better, and dismissed
     His fears, a foolish optimist.
     Might she, her fam'ly, have availed him?
     No wonder that he's acting strange,
     And lied to her about the change.
     He'd needed help and she had failed him.
     She feels, that chance now long gone by,
     At last too hollowed-out to cry.

31. "He can't remember," from behind her
     The Gräfin says, her pale arms crossed.
     Her words sound sadder. Almost kinder.
     "Some portions of his mind were lost
     When he endured his transformation.
     But take it as a consolation
     That any pain was worth the trade.
     The little sacrifices made
     Don't matter." She continues, smugly,
     "It's done now and, if I were you,
     I'd move on and forget him too."
     In Kinge something raw and ugly
     Wells up and turns her vision black.
     She doesn't try to hold it back.

32. Her heel against the flooring screeches
    As she spins round to bring her foe
    Within her line of sight. She reaches
    Inside her jacket for…but no.
    The holster's empty, and the weapon
    Was locked away ere she could step in
    The castle. Standard protocol.
    The Gräfin's laughter fills the hall.
    "Be careful. I, like you, live under
    His lordship's aegis. He would take
    It poorly if you were to make
    A move against me, Kunigunde."
    She bares her teeth. "Or have you, dear,
    Forgotten I am Gräfin here?"

33. These two, despite the hatred in their
    Expressions, halt when Kinge sees
    That Timoch (how long has he been there?)
    Is watching them. He stands at ease
    But eyes them dangerously, mutely,
    And Kinge steps back. Resolutely
    She squares her shoulders, breathes, collects
    Herself. Then, cooly, she directs
    These words toward the Gräfin: "All that
    You say is true. Perhaps. I don't
    Have means to fight you, and I won't,
    Not now. But if he should recall that
    Protection, watch your back. Because
    I will destroy you when he does."

34. The Gräfin puffs with indignation,
    But Kinge sees a muscle twitch.
    Or is it her imagination?
    The vampire, scared? A welcome switch.
    Her eyelids closed to narrow slivers,
    The Gräfin perfectly delivers
    An undead monster's evil eye.
    "Oh, little girl," she says, "you'll try."
    Then, smiling once again, she glances
    At Timoch, who returns her no
    Attention, like he doesn't owe
    Her any. Swiftly she advances
    Past both of them and off she goes,
    A whiff of myrrh in Kinge's nose.

35. It's Timoch—brisk, unsentimental—
    Who breaks the quiet. "Time to leave,"
    He says. And yet his touch is gentle,
    His fingers pressing on her sleeve
    As he escorts her. She, still shaken,
    Is worried that she will be taken
    To task for what she might have done
    Had he not locked away her gun,
    But he says nothing to accuse her.
    The two move swiftly through the lair
    And silently, as if aware
    That any further talk would bruise her,
    He takes her where her things are stored,
    Cold comfort all he may afford.

36. Towards the car she heads out, shrugging
    Against the cool air. Suddenly
    She feels, about her heart, a tugging
    That slows her steps. Reluctantly
    She turns, and her emotions ravel.
    Her eyes along the turrets travel
    And up to where, absurdly high,
    The tower punctuates the sky.
    She cannot pinpoint how she knows this
    To look upon that pile of stones,
    But she can feel it in her bones:
    The Graf is there. It's like he chose this
    Prime spot to watch the ground below
    And, from a distance, see her go.

37. The tugging at her heart grows fiercer.
    She could go back, climb up the stair…
    She doesn't, though such longings pierce her.
    She knows that isn't why he's there.
    He doesn't mount that lofty spire
    Because he has some deep desire
    To watch what happens on the ground.
    He's on that tower to surround
    Himself with stars and stand among them.
    He told her once, one summer night,
    How he drew solace from their light,
    As if the Lord Himself had hung them
    To give immortal creatures peace
    When other forms of comfort cease.

38. She's stung by this, betrayed, offended
     That his attention elsewhere lies
     With their affair but newly ended.
     It isn't fair. But then, she tries
     To see the sky from his perspective.
     Its stars and planets, in collective,
     Majestic patterns wildly strung,
     Look as they have since he was young
     And as they will for ages longer.
     There's power in their constancy,
     And Kunigunde finds that she
     From their light feels her own grow stronger,
     That veil of brilliant points a scrim
     Behind all she has learned from him.

39. To know the calm of deathless skies is
     The vampire's final, finest gift,
     Beyond the other things he prizes:
     His library, his name. She lifts
     Her eyes and sees the faintest shimmer
     Atop the tow'r. Could that be him, or
     A trick of light? Perhaps she's wrong,
     And he's been watching all along.
     Imperfect solace, then. His vigil,
     It changes nothing, now. It can't.
     But never will the Graf recant
     A promise made that bore his sigil.
     Recalling what he once had vowed,
     "Until they're dust," she says aloud.

40. She stops to readjust her pistol
Within its holster, takes her key
And starts the car. As clear as crystal,
But dark, this night. Her path will be
The same. But she can make it brighter,
Somehow. She'll be a fairer fighter
Than Hellers gone before, and still
Beware the vampires' natures. She'll
Remember Galen. So much sorrow
And hope for her to reconcile.
It hurts, and will do for a while.
For now—her classes start tomorrow.
She'll need her rest when that arrives.
She puts the car in gear, and drives.

THE END

"For His Ghost"—A Dedication

I promised that I wouldn't write you
Again until my book was done.
And then, with pride, would I invite you
To read the verses I had spun,
In hopes that you might find them moving.
Perhaps you'd see your health improving
Enough a concert tour to wage,
So I could see you on the stage!
For this I watched, and prayed, and waited.
Alas, the lines of fate were drawn.
One autumn morning you were gone,
And I was simply devastated.
So now I set myself to rhyme
Some verse for you, one final time.

I'll never have the joy of hearing
Your voice in person. That still burns.
Nor see you act a role, appearing
Aloof and passionate by turns.
A part of me already misses
You taking bows and blowing kisses,
Exuding humor, grace, and style.
My heart would burst to see your smile.
Well, there will be no more ovations,
White roses at the curtain call.
You're finite, now. But aren't we all?
Though, quite despite my lamentations,
You've sung all you will ever sing,
There yet remains, perhaps, one thing.

For all my dashed hopes and frustration
This year, my writing grows apace.
You live in my imagination;
My novel's hero has your face
And smiles like you. Although I'm saddened
You'll never see my book, I'm gladdened
To think a reader might, some day,
Be moved by it in much the way
Your work moves me. In such a fashion
I think I might effectively
Do justice to your memory.
Thank you for all your art and passion.
I'm grateful more than words can tell.
Good-bye, my genius. Rest you well.

Acknowledgments

So many people supported me as I wrote this story. I would especially like to thank:

The team at Lanternfish Press. Christine Neulieb's thoughtful critiques helped me make this book stronger.

The South Shore Scribes, who listened to this story unfold in four-stanza segments across nearly two years and made me believe the story could find an audience. Special thanks are due Christine Lajewski, who encouraged me to write my story in this form and has supported me every step of the way.

Chris Degni, who, in addition to his excellent feedback, counted all my syllables. He is a really useful engine.

Chris Johnson, who hosted socially distant get-togethers in his backyard.

Heather J. Randolph, who pointed out plot inconsistencies and helped keep me sane.

Vesna Gronosky, who lent me her expertise with German grammar and Serbian names.

Doug Beeferman, who helped me out when something went wrong with my computer and RhymeZone stopped working.

And finally my husband, Hunter Keeton. He read every stanza as I wrote it, told me I had to finish the book, and looked after the kids while I did.

About the Author

JESSICA LÉVAI has loved stories and storytellers for as long as she can remember. After a PhD in Egyptology and eight years as a professor of Anthropology, she dedicated herself to writing full time. She lives near Boston with her husband and two kids.

.